PANGS OF AN
ENTOMOLOGIST

Pangs of an Entomologist

Dr. Debashis Biswas

PARTRIDGE
A Penguin Random House Company

ISBN: Softcover   978-1-4828-1459-0
            Ebook   978-1-4828-1458-3

Cover: Suvendu Sur

To order additional copies of this book, contact
Partridge India
000 800 10062 62
www.partridgepublishing.com/india
orders.india@partridgepublishing.com

DEDICATION

I am dedicating the 'Pangs of an Entomologist' to all those state health ministers, members of legislative assembly, members of parliament, city mayors and councillors of municipal corporations in India, who, for a genuine reason of their utter unawareness about the subject, are still inclined to believe that mosquito control is a trivial job and hence do not bother to know as to how the government-sponsored activities with regard to mosquito-bashing programme are going on in their constituencies to prevent transmission of malaria, dengue, lymphatic filariasis and other mosquito-borne diseases.

ACKNOWLEDGEMENTS

Atin Ghosh, Member of the Mayor-in-Council (Health & Engineering) of Kolkata Municipal Corporation, for revolutionising mosquito control activities in the city of Kolkata by employing the services of Entomologists to the fullest extent.

Debasis Som (IAS), former Municipal Commissioner of KMC, for giving me the official nod to use a hired car for official work.

Bikashranjan Bhattacharya, former city Mayor, for saying 'yes' to deployment of three Consultant Entomologists on a contractual basis.

Alapan Bandyopadhyay (IAS), former Municipal Commissioner of KMC, for fixing the monthly remuneration of each Consultant Entomologist at par with that of a Medical Officer.

Tapas Chowdhury (WBCS), former Joint Municipal Commissioner (Development) of KMC, for enhancing the remuneration of a Consultant Entomologist always in tune with that of a Medical Officer despite severe opposition by the medical fraternity of the corporation.

My colleagues—Atanu, Baishakhi, Bithika and Deba— for helping me resolve official problems.

Mohimarnab, my son, for reading between the lines of the manuscript.

Rahul, younger brother, for providing miscellaneous support at times of dire need.

Mousumi, my wife, for creating the ambience I urgently needed to write this book.

Contents

Pangs of Munda 1

Only Munda knew it 12

Munda's trust stabbed 22

Munda spent half an hour with a doctor's ladder 42

Is Munda the man to visit burning ghats??? 46

Munda's slip of tongue 49

Munda's concern about JE 59

Doctors' dereliction 63

Panja's pride pricked by a doctor 67

Munda's leaflet messed up by doctors 71

Sir, forgive them, they're your brethren 75

Voice for mosquitoes 78

Gorgas: the unsung hero 81

Oman conquers malaria 85

Pregnancy attracts mosquitoes 88

Human transport of dengue 95

Dengue does not annoy them 98

Preventing dengue 103

Power of politics 108

Man smart, mosquito smarter 112

How we help mosquitoes breed 119

LLIN is more protective 130

Talk show on mosquito repellents 135

Munda's inputs for you 143

Munda's prescription 151
Mosquito control is everybody's responsibility 155
A leader's fight against mosquitoes................................ 166
Eye of a mosquito counsellor.. 186
Hriday and Madhu.. 191
Deaf bureaucracy 198
Lessons from a leader of mosquitoes 203
Entomologists can give it a crack 209
Devastating 1997... 217

ALSO BY DR. DEBASHIS BISWAS

Maleria Ki Keno O Tar Mokabila

Masha

Masha Banam Mashababu

The Sting

Dengue Resurgence

Maye Maleria Daye Dengi

Basics of Mosquitoes

Pangs of Munda

Dr Animesh Munda (original name changed) is an entomologist (expert in the subject of insects). Some of his friends fondly call him "mashababu" (mosquito-man). He works in the health department of Beldanga Municipal Corporation (BMC). And he is a very busy man, so much so that he cannot spend time with his family. He works even on Sundays, forgetting all his social attachment. While the rest of the city is busy talking business, watching TV or enjoying a day-out, Munda is engaged in accomplishing his official tasks. Unlike his senior officers, who feel their duty is restricted to a 10 to 5 schedule, Munda's battle goes on.

Even his harsh critics will admit that Munda's contribution as an individual overrides his capacity as a civic employee. His take on an allegedly "dry job" is interesting. "After completing my schooling in a remote village of North Bengal, I came to Calcutta for higher studies. After doing BSc (Honours) in zoology at a most ordinary college, I did masters in the same subject at Calcutta University. Before I could contemplate any other option, a scholarship for a junior researcher at a renowned research institute came my way. I needed money, so I started research on mosquitoes. And I got the degree of PhD from Calcutta University for my thesis on the bionomics of the dengue-bearing mosquito *Aedes aegypti*," briefs Munda, no pride in his voice about his achievements.

Over the years, his untiring official work has not reduced the passion within the "mosquito-man". In the past 20 years, he has written more than 100 stories in both Bengali and English in reputed dailies and 7 books, all for people's awareness. But the department of BMC he has long been working with treats him as a mere duty-bound employee. His bosses cash in on his service but lack the will to respect him. Since Munda is not a medical man, health officials of his department always treat him as an enemy of theirs.

There are five deputy chief municipal health officers (Dy CMHOs) and fifteen borough executive health officers (Br Ex HOs) in the health department of BMC, who, in spite of having no or very little knowledge about the subject, look after mosquito control activities in different wards of BMC through medical officers (MOs). Interestingly, Dy CMHOs and Br Ex HOs are all seniors to Dr Munda.

The area of BMC consists of 144 wards. Mosquito control work in each ward is looked after by an MO. The MOs are accountable to their Br Ex HOs. The Br Ex HOs are answerable to their Dy CMHOs and the Dy

CMHOs are accountable to the CMHO (chief municipal health officer). Clearly, Dr Animesh Munda (MSc, PhD) is a no-man in the hierarchy of the health department of BMC. He is a very small fish in a big pond. To the doctors of BMC, Munda is just a non-medical staff, nothing else and nothing more.

In BMC, Munda acts as a playback singer. He sings for Jagannath Panja, member of the mayor-in-council (Health). He sings for Shakil Ahmed, municipal commissioner. He sings for Dr Nirjan Baker, CMHO. He sings for his immediate boss Dr Koutilya Makal, Dy CMHO and OSD (Health). They move their lips very consciously, get patted by the audience and forget Munda's assistance. They cash in on Munda's service but feel shaky to disclose the truth when it comes to expressing indebtedness to him. Having served such self-centred people over the years, Munda has lost his faith in BMC administration. He does not like to work there any more. He wants to resign from his post. But a feeling of insecurity holds him back from taking any harsh decision. He is now 52 plus. Where will Munda go at this age? If he quits, he will face dire consequences. He needs money for his son Rahul. Rahul reads in class XII at a private school where the fee rockets up every now and then.

Munda has no way to escape his duties. He spends 9-10 hours per day for his department. And the tasks he accomplishes are huge and painstaking. Jagannath Panja, MMIC (Health) has of late asked Koutilya to look after the administration of Munda's office. But Koutilya is not at all serious about his assignment. He comes to Munda's office once or twice a month and spends some time talking all gobbledygook to Munda and other employees of the office. Munda and other staff of his office feel disturbed by the arrival of Makal.

Makal is a self-important man. For reasons best known to him, he misbehaves with Munda. Like all his predecessors, he is also very sly. He knows how to pass the buck to others. If any problem concerning Munda's office is brought to his notice, Makal asks Munda at once to work it out and submit an action-taken report to him. Munda thought Makal would help him concentrate more on entomological activities and honestly try to resolve day-to-day problems of his office himself after becoming the head of his office. But this is not happening. Things are going wrong. Munda's workload has increased. Munda still looks after each and every petty issue of his office. Most of his activities are not commensurate with his designation. As an entomologist, Munda's main and only duty is to plan and implement need-based strategies for mosquito abatement to prevent the transmission of mosquito-borne diseases in the city. But Munda can't do this in BMC. The health authority of BMC does not allow him to perform the job of an entomologist. The department keeps him engaged in some other activities which do not come under Munda's purview.

What the hell does Dr Koutilya Makal do then for Munda's office? One of the best ever dialogues in the history of Hollywood comes from Uncle Parker who, in one of the films of the monstrously successful franchise— The Spiderman—tells Peter, "With great power comes great responsibility." This philosophy is exactly what the monster, Koutilya, doesn't believe in. Koutilya is someone who takes the crown, enjoys the power but backs out just when a little responsibility is needed to be taken. Why has Mr Panja made him the boss of Munda's office? The question haunts everyone working in the office of Munda.

By making Dr Makal the boss of Munda, the MMIC (Health), Mr Panja, has committed a great blunder and he will have to pay a lot for this very soon. Munda and his team of consultant entomologists, for reasons still unknown to them, are getting humiliated by Makal, a secret story that Jagannath Panja does not know. Mr Panja even does not know how, by way of insulting them, Makal is tactfully demoralising Munda and his team of entomologists, the consequence of which will be disastrous.

But who will report to Mr Panja against Dr Makal? Cracking the relationship between Makal and Mr Panja is very tough. About a month ago, sitting beside Mr Panja, Dr Baker, CMHO, simply pointed out one mistake made by Dr Makal. Mr Panja's face turned grim in a jiffy. He admonished Dr Baker. Mr Panja has a profound faith in Makal. He trusts Makal. He respects Makal. And he considers him as a very efficient health officer. Makal seems to have hypnotised him. He is now sleeping. Let's wait and watch. Makal is Panja's baby. So, Mr Panja will face the consequence. Unmasking his venomous baby is not needed.

Sitting in his office, what does Munda do for BMC? Munda does a lot of work. He signs monthly wage bills of contractually engaged field workers, salary bills of all staff of his office, vouchers and contingency bills. He signs monthly bills for hired vehicles. He signs personal files and service books of different employees of his office. If supply of water to his office suddenly stops, he helps restore it. He provides transport to different borough health offices for carrying insecticides, equipment, furniture, medicines and other such materials from the Central Stores of BMC. The list is endless.

There are three consultant entomologists in the office of Munda. They work as per the plans and guidelines of Munda. Munda analyses mosquito-related data collected by entomologists from fields and submits reports to Mr Panja, Dr Baker and Dr Makal on a weekly basis. The health department of BMC has of late established a research laboratory to study population dynamics of the disease spreading mosquitoes of Beldanga. Day-to-day activities in this mosquito research laboratory run under the supervision of Munda. Planning of studies, analysis of research inputs and publication of research papers in medical journals are all done by Munda.

Around nine hundred contractually engaged field workers (FWs) now work in different wards of the city. The tenure of contractual engagement of these FWs is renewed at different periods of time and Munda, the branded scapegoat, is the person to draft proposals needed for renewing their term of engagement. Sometimes queries concerning deployment of these FWs come to him for clarification. And that too is done by him.

Imparting training on mosquito control is another piece of work that Munda organises with the help of consultant entomologists. Ward MOs, FWs and other categories of employees benefit by his training. Mosquito control personnel from some other non-BMC organisations such as the railways department, state health department and other municipalities too now come to Munda to learn about the nitty-gritty of mosquito abatement.

Multicoloured leaflets, hoardings, banners, booklets and posters containing do's and don'ts for prevention of mosquito-borne diseases are now brought out by the corporation every year to send out messages against malaria and dengue for people's awareness. Who drafts these publicity materials for the department? It's nobody else, but our Munda.

In 2011, a document-based multicoloured booklet on mosquitoes and mosquito-borne diseases was published by BMC. Over three lakh copies of this booklet were distributed among the school students of as many as seven hundred schools of the city for their awareness. The idea of publishing such booklet was the brainchild of Jagannath Panja. But, together with Dr Baker, Munda had to work hard to materialise the idea of Mr Panja, and only Dr Baker knows how much sweat Munda had to shed for bringing out the booklet. He drafted the manuscript in consultation with Dr Baker and did proof-reading. Photographs used in the booklet too were provided by him. Initially, the booklet was drafted in English. Then it was translated into Bengali, Hindi and Urdu. Translation of the booklet from English to Bengali was done by Munda. Neither any Dy CMHO nor any Br Ex HO helped him get such tedious work done.

Munda's lecture on mosquitoes has some demand in the market. The concerned faculty members of a renowned medical institute requests him every year to deliver a lecture on his subject before the doctors doing the course of diploma in public health (DPH, in short). Munda accepts their invitation and spends 2-3 hours with the DPH students helping them learn about mosquito control.

Insecticides, knapsack sprayers and fogging machines are very essential for mosquito control workers of the health department of BMC to carry out their activities across the city. Who helps them get timely supply of all these materials? Dr Animesh Munda. Munda collects requisitions from different boroughs of BMC, compiles them singlehandedly and sends the final requisition to the concerned department for an early procurement. Spare parts needed to repair knapsack sprayers and fogging machines are also caused to be brought in by him. And who looks after the distribution of these materials among different borough health offices? It's our Munda, again.

Sometimes reports concerning the BMC's activities with regard to prevention and control of mosquito-borne diseases (malaria, dengue, chikungunya, etc) are sought by the directorate of the NVBDCP (National Vector Borne Disease Control Programme), Government of India, and the state health department. Who helps BMC draft and send such reports? It's nobody else, but Munda. Following the implementation of the Right to Information act, citizens of the country are increasingly becoming conscious about their rights. People's queries on malaria and dengue control activities now frequently come in to BMC and Munda helps the corporation reply and dispatch those queries on time.

In the city of Beldanga, there are many sewerage canals and these canals are a big source of *Culex* mosquito. To keep the mosquito menace under control, the health department of BMC has been doing larvicidal spray along the edges of these canals since 2011 by using small rowing-boats as transport. And Munda is the only man to look after this project.

Drafting affidavits concerning each and every Public Interest Litigation on mosquito control activities of the health department of BMC is another painstaking job done by Munda alone, following the order of CMHO. And by submitting his write-ups to the Honourable High Court, the department wins cases, but the department does not recognise Munda's contribution.

Sometimes instructions for drafting letters, communiqués and office orders come down to Munda from the municipal commissioner of BMC through CMHO. The unfortunate mosquito-man complies with the instructions like an obedient boy.

These apart, drafting annual action plan for prevention and control of malaria and dengue, steering activities of 21 newly formed Rapid Action Squads for mosquito control, providing technical inputs to his bosses on matters relating to mosquito control as and when required, drafting performance report of the health department, making arrangements for displaying photographs and other such publicity materials against mosquito-borne diseases in Health Fairs organised by any government or a non-government organisation and participating in chat shows on mosquito abatement, malaria, dengue, etc on behalf of the health department of BMC are also done by Munda.

Unfortunately, Munda has no future. He works in such a post that has no promotional scope. The health department of BMC has made his post crippled. He joined BMC as an entomologist about two-and-half-decades ago. He still works as an entomologist. And he will retire as an entomologist. The duties and responsibilities of this easy-to-annoy mosquito-man have increased manifold. But the official rank of Munda's post has still been kept below the rank of a borough executive health officer.

The most demoralising part of the story is that a medical officer of BMC has the privilege to enjoy an additional benefit of the Career Advancement Scheme after completing 26 years of service, apart from enjoying two subsequent benefits—one after completion of 10 years of service and one after completion of 20 years of service. But Animesh Munda will never get the additional benefit of the CAS after completion of 26 years of service since he is an MSc-PhD and not an MBBS. Clearly, after shouldering so many responsibilities over a period of long 26 years, the official rank of Munda will come down to a rank lower than that of a medical officer of BMC. What a system!

In 2009, three consultant entomologists were deployed by the corporation on a contractual basis and Munda's post was redesignated as the chief entomologist without according any financial benefit against the uplift. His uplift was non-promotional. Deputy municipal commissioner Kameshwar Bandyopadhyay, who looks after the personnel department of BMC, could have done something for Munda. But he did not. Munda still works in the same rank as was on the day of his joining BMC.

On 14 July 2011, Munda wrote a letter to the then municipal commissioner of BMC, Raghu Roy, IAS, urging him to uplift his post at least to the rank of a Br Ex HO so that he could smoothly visit different wards of BMC and monitor the activities of all categories of staff, including the ward MOs, with regard to mosquito control. Copies of the letter were sent to the city mayor, MMIC (Health), joint municipal commissioner, CMHO and Dy CMHO & OSD (Health). But the unfortunate Munda is still awaiting their response.

A staggering 24 years have disappeared from the life of Munda. His blood is getting colder. The countdown for him has begun and Munda is preparing himself for his unceremonious departure from the devastating Black Building of Beldanga Municipal Corporation.

ONLY MUNDA KNEW IT

On 21 June 2013, a team of three doctors from the state health department dropped in on Dr Nirjan Baker, chief municipal health officer (CMHO) of BMC (Beldanga Municipal Corporation), to assure him of a government aid of Rs 95,00,000 to step up mosquito control activities in the city of Beldanga for prevention and control of malaria and dengue. A day later, in the late evening, Ms Anopheles Gambiae (AG), malaria-bearing mosquito of Africa, winged into a dark public urinal at a corner of the lawn of BMC headquarters as the Chief Guest of a session called by flustered females of the city's malaria-spreading community Anopheles Stephensi (AS).

Ms AG alighted to the raucous grating of proboscis against proboscis (proboscis is a needle-like appendage by which a mosquito pierces our skin to imbibe blood). Minutes later, serious business was got down to. Ms AG was called upon to make a speech and the sleek, grey, dappled-winged professional got right down to business. "Dear demoralised comrades of Beldanga, I'll not waste your time with irrelevancies. Let's dwell on what we are and the strength we possess. We emerged on this earth long, long before humans did, and we know how to face odds and threats. Resisting each and every heinous human invasion, we still manage very well, grabbing more and more to add to our domain.

"Over 30,00,00,000 people around the world now fall prey to our attacks every year and 10,00,000 of them die. The parasite that causes the deadly version of malaria is called PF (read *Plasmodium falciparum*) and we inject this very killer germ into the blood of most Africans. Nearly one-third of these global deaths occur among the children below five. And you will be delighted to know that days ahead will be ours. People who plan tricks to destroy our community have already issued an alert that as a sequel to global warming and climate changes, the hitherto inimical places like the southern part of the United States of America as well as the southern part of Europe too will in near future become conducive to our procreation and many people there will fall victim to our attacks every year . . ."

"Bravo, bravo, bravo . . ." rasped her appreciative audience.

"Silence!" Ms AG boomed and proceeded to continue in now shrill tone. "In Africa, we kill people in lakhs. Our sting in that continent is feared. But out here in Beldanga, your performance is downright frustrating. In 2010, nearly 0.1 million people of this city became afflicted with the germ of malaria. The figure came down to 46000 in 2011. In 2012, it stood at a frustrating 32000. Shame, shame, shame! Why has your performance dwindled so alarmingly? Huh? I need explanation from the convener of this session. Now. Right now."

Ms AS, convener, who was sitting beside Ms AG, shrivelled at the rebuke. "But, Madam, I mean . . ."

"What do you mean?" Ms Gambiae shot back. "The truth, Ms AS . . ."

"It's all due to Varunda's negligence, Madam," Ms AS complained after a brief pause. "Had he been a bit more cooperative, the scenario would have been much better. He betrayed us . . ."

"Who's that bastard?" Ms AG thundered.

"The God of Rains, Ma'am," Ms AS enlightened her. "In 2009, there were 1604 mm of rainfall. But in 2010, that celestial idiot sent down only 1440 mm. So our usual procreation in Beldanga was greatly hampered and hence that was why . . ."

"And how much did your Varunda give you in 2011 and 2012?" demanded Ms AG, rolling her multifaceted eyes (read compound eyes) vigorously.

"S-sorry, Ma'am," Ms AS stuttered. "A-actually, I mean . . ."

"Shut up," the international leader kicked her in the back. "You've purposely dropped the figures for the next two years to bemuse me, idiot! I know this city thousand times better than you. Listen. In 2011, the amount was 1579 mm, clearly 139 mm more than in 2010. In 2012 too, Varunbabu gifted you a good amount, it was 1577 mm. Still you couldn't improve performance of your community."

So saying, Ms Gambiae buzzed around Ms Stephensi for some while and then, goggling at her, mocked, "While receiving me at the mayor's gate of this Black Building, you told me that your community was the No 1 group of terrorists in Beldanga. Am I to believe your words any more?"

At this humiliation, the audience of Ms AS broke into sobs. Red-faced with shame, some of the females tried to protest, but the tricky African leader soon shut them up. "Don't bother raising the roof. I know exactly what's happening in this Beldanga. You are not at all doing your job meticulously. Remember, next time, I won't tolerate this dereliction. I want our enemies' massacre, at any cost, understand?" Then with peremptory thanks for their attention, Ms AG took wing, headed back for Africa with the parting shot that she expected a better performance.

Apparently much distressed, the convener of the conference, Ms AS, rose to speak. "My dear comrades, perhaps our learned Chief Guest wasn't aware that we have long been struggling against rather heavy odds here in Beldanga. The use of DDT in the late 1950s killed millions of our comrades. We had to lie low for some years but then we learnt to digest this poison.

"To bypass the threats of insecticides, we have changed our behaviour too. Now, instead of resting on the walls and ceilings of households, our female cadres wait outside, drop in for dinner and take their leave. Today we're bolder, fatter, hardier and smarter than ever before.

"And man, our great enemy, has made us more virulent." Switching tirade in the general direction of the mayor of BMC, Gopiballabh Chatterjee, Ms AS continued, "Mr Mayor, you may wipe out the tiger and the elephant, whose reproductive potential is relatively small, but you simply can't get rid of us. Our trump card lies in our ability to develop a super-quick resistance. We bite your citizens at night. During the day we lurk in dark humid places, behind almirahs, damp clothes, in empty earthen pitchers and drums, below wooden cots and other such places.

"However, our children (read larvae) haven't learnt the art of camouflage. Because they grow in open water containers in and around human-dwellings, they're easily detected by the anti-mosquito squads of the corporation and brutally done in. But thanks to some city-dwellers' deep sense of philanthropy, some of our hapless and helpless kids are safe. They manage to tide over the larval stage in water containers that human foster-parents leave conveniently alone. Promoters, developers, officers-in-charge of some police stations, authorities of educational institutes, superintendents of government hospitals, caretakers of office buildings here are all damn good people. They are magnanimous. Despite being repeatedly provoked by the corporation people, they don't flair up against us. Had they been ruthless and non-cooperative, our community would have been wiped out.

"But hard times are again upon us," and here Ms AS choked causing a flutter of nervousness to invade her audience. "What's up? What did you mean?" they asked.

"Our lives are not safe," Ms AS replied in a pensive voice. "The newly joined member of the mayor-in-council (Health) of BMC, Jagannath Panja, is a very sly fellow. Mr Panja is out to kill us at our source. He is a great provocateur. Besides asking all categories of employees of his health department to strengthen the drive for elimination of our community, Mr Panja is now asking the innocent people of Beldanga in different ways to revolt against us.

"Know too that the BMC's entomologist Dr Animesh Munda and his team of 3 consultant entomologists are our only professional killers in this city. To my utter astonishment, Jagannath Panja has given them free hands to mount an all-out drive in every nook and corner of the city to kill our kids. By detailing their accomplices in different wards of BMC, they are now murdering our kids in millions. Following the instructions of Mr Panja, that rascal Munda is now sending out all dangerous anti-Stephensi messages through booklets, leaflets, banners and hoardings. As a result, some people who once were our dedicated caretakers have taken to checking their water containers at weekly intervals—which does not bode well for our community since we emerge from the egg in a week or a bit more. They are spending crores of rupees to stir up the people's ire against our offspring.

"The MMIC (Health) is a very notorious murderer. He's trying to wipe out our community from Beldanga. He has established a laboratory to collect information about us. Field workers of BMC, who, for a reason of their inability to identify our children (read mosquito larvae), once used to spray costly poison here and there in the name of killing our kids, now come to Jagannath's laboratory on a regular basis to see our children lying trapped in enamel trays. Most of them can now identify our kids quite easily. Comrades, this is not a good indication. If they all learn about identification of our kids, we are finished."

Having said this, Ms AS stopped for a while and then, looking around with a wry smile, began, "Jagannath Panja hates our community. People around him still cannot read his mind. He believes nobody. He is unpredictable. I have never seen such a cruel mosquito hater ever before. A tall obese man in his mid-fifties is now organising devastating raids to destroy our labour rooms across the city. About 3 years ago, the situation was totally different. The city's previous member of the mayor-in-council (Health), Dr Nishikanta Dey, was a genuine gentleman. He was a poor-friendly doctor. There is a wide-spread rumour that Nishikanta's love for the poor was so intense that he did not bother to tie his second marriage-knot with an ugly cherry-black housemaid soon after his first wife, who was an educated elite, had burnt herself alive."

Having said this, Ms AS stopped, gave rest to her voice for a while and then, after rolling her small compound eyes clockwise and anticlockwise for 3-4 rounds, continued, "Sitting almost idle in his spacious AC chamber, Dr Dey spent a long five years from June 2005 to May 2010 without causing any harm to our members. Taking suggestions from some tainted doctors of his department, the man in his late-seventies kept Munda confined in a small dark room about 1.5 km away from the headquarters of BMC.

"Munda's advice had no value to him. Since he was deaf, he used to listen to his visitors without using the hearing aid. He was a real friend of ours. In those five years of his régime in the Black Building of BMC, he called Munda hardly for 5-6 times. Nishikantada was a python. He used to engulf his prey silently, leaving no trace behind. He was a perfect Bangalibabu. Always he used to communicate in Bengali but people could not understand his language.

"His was a unique style of speaking. Like other doctors of his department, Dr Dey too was in favour of treating patients of malaria rather than preventing transmission of the disease. He opened many malaria clinics across the city. It was a golden time for us. The entire BMC building was ours. In one room of the Black Building, there was Dr Nishikanta Dey, and in another room, there was Dr Dashanan Das—what a combination! It was as if the Almighty had sent the duo to protect our community against the hostile forces. With the tacit support of Nishikantada, Dashanan earned lakhs of rupees by deploying many inefficient laboratory technicians at the malaria clinics of BMC.

"According to Nishikantada, treatment is always better than prevention. But Mr Panja is a different breed. Panja does not believe in treatment. He believes only in destroying us. 'Prevention is better than cure' is his only motto. And he has been sending out this provocative message to all people around him since he joined the BMC in June 2010. But don't lose hearts, dear comrades. The days of the monster are numbered. Some leaders of his own party are now out to tarnish his image. The brute now feels what a blunder he had committed during 2010 to 2012 by slashing the burden of malaria in Beldanga. Since the other MMICs of BMC have not yet been able to make their presence felt by the city-dwellers, they have all become jealous of Jagannath's fame. As far as my knowledge goes, Mr Panja will not get the portfolio of MMIC (Health) next time even if his party wins the civic election in 2015. Just wait and watch. Our favourite Beldanga will be freed from the grip of Jagannath soon. By the way, I have one intriguing news to share with you. But don't disclose it to anybody else. Listen carefully."

The audience turned curious. "What, Didi?"

Ms AS looked sideways and then in a very low voice, said, "Dr Koutilya Makal is already in. He is our new custodian. He has two faces, one to delude Jagannath Panja and one to abuse our professional killers—Munda and his team of entomologists. He will finish them very soon. He believes only in equation of convenience. The two dedicated officials of BMC, Dr Nirjan Baker and Dr Animesh Munda, who have worked hard for more than three years since 2010 as the advisers to Jagannath Panja and made him famous in the field of malaria containment in the city of Beldanga, are now slowly snapping their ties with him. Our story, I mean, the story of the beginning of an era of our peaceful procreation across Beldanga, will begin soon. Makal hates both Baker and Munda . . ."

Before unfurling her dappled wings, Ms AS praised the crowd with an ecstatic smile, "Beldanga has been in our grip since its inception. And contrary to the perception of our venerated AG Madam, our Stephensi community in Beldanga is performing very well. And from 2015, we will show her how ferocious the females of our community are. So far we have killed more than 400 people here since 1993. So don't feel humiliated by her comment. Just keep it up. You'll certainly do much better in the years to come. Take care. Good-bye."

The meeting over, the swarm of tiny winged terrorists began to disperse. Most females flew into the bedrooms of a nearby gorgeous multi-storey building to imbibe blood from the people sleeping on their costly beds completely unprotected. The rest of them, especially the pregnant ones, went to the rooftop of the BMC building on a different mission.

The day before, there had been a heavy downpour in the city of Beldanga (110.6 mm), as a result of which some 5-6 empty paint containers—which had for the past several days been lying stacked at a corner of the roof of the building—became filled with rainwater. The gravid females came close to the containers, sat on their brims, smile-faced, and then, after rolling their eyes for some while, winged into them to lay their eggs undisturbed.

Munda's trust stabbed

Instance one

It was in the late 2003 or the early 2004. About one month after his brother-in-law had died an awful death in a road accident in North Bengal, Dr Koutilya Makal, the then borough executive health officer of BMC (Beldanga Municipal Corporation), suddenly dropped in at the office of Dr Animesh Munda, entomologist, and sobbed, "The life of my beloved sister has been ruined. She's now just 35. With one daughter and one son, what will she do now? Baba and Ma want her to come to Beldanga and stay with them forever . . ."

"Don't lose hearts, Makalda," Munda pacified him. "We are with you. Your sister is our sister. Tell her not to feel alone." Having said this, Munda took out a sheet of paper from his drawer and began to draft an application to be submitted by Koutilya to the CM of the state of Jhautala urging him to help his nephew get an early admission to a good Bengali-medium boys' high school in Beldanga, preferably a government-run school in the southern part of the city. Putting all his pre-scheduled official assignments unaccomplished, Munda spent the whole day drafting the application for Makal and listening to kitchen stories of his family.

Two days later, Munda talked to a Private Secretary of the CM over telephone, intimated to him the heart-rending story of Koutilya's sister and requested him to deal with the case personally, giving a top priority. "Of course, I will do," the PS assured instantaneously. A beatific smile crossed the chickenpox-scarred face of Munda.

The PS kept his words. Instructions from the Hon'ble CM to process the case on a war-footing reached the Education Department 5-6 days later. Admission of Koutilya's nephew to a renowned government boys' high school (named Beldanga Boys' Institution), located very near to his house, was recommended by the CM himself.

A close relative of Munda was working in the Education Department at that time. Hence getting the official order issued to the headmaster of the school specified by the CM became easier. The order came out within a week's time and the process of the child's admission was completed quite smoothly. And the entire family of Koutilya heaved a sigh of relief.

The first agenda over, he sought another help from Munda. He said, "My sister now badly needs to get her widow pension and other financial benefits from the state health department at an early date. Please do help. I know you have good connections with some officials working in that department."

"Leave it to me. I will handle this issue," Munda assured him.

Munda personally met the CA (confidential assistant) to the state health minister taking reference from a renowned political leader and then talked to Dr Nikhilesh Mukherjee, officer-in-charge of the pension cell of doctors of the health department, about the issue of Koutilya's sister.

One day, Koutilya said to Munda, "Mukherjee is very rude. He's my next-door neighbour. He has a personal grudge against me and our family. I don't know why he misbehaves with me. I won't meet him alone. Would you please accompany me?"

"Sure," Munda acquiesced. "I will go with you. Not to worry . . ."

Munda did the job religiously. He met Nikhilesh once along with Dr Makal. Thereafter, he personally met him thrice. Besides, he phoned him 4-5 times to do the follow-ups and used all his personal connections to bring about a reconciliation between the two docs, but failed. One day, Munda met Nikhilesh alone, gifted him two books authored by himself and deceived him by flatteries. The trick worked wonders. The anger of Nikhilesh against the doctor of BMC got pacified and he personally helped his sister get her widow pension in a very short span of time.

Munda became Makal's younger brother overnight. Telephonic chat between the two employees of BMC began. On every alternate day, he used to call up the mosquito-man after 11 o'clock in the night and tell him the stories all about him, his wife, daughter and father-in-law. Interestingly, the bulk of his mid-night story used to revolve mostly round the unlimited treasure of his father-in-law. In Beldanga, he used to say, his father-in-law was such a rich man that he could buy any part of the city at the wink of an eye. Animesh used to digest all those repetitive trash silently. It was never about the entomologist on the phone. It was always the doctor. It was always his family. Gradually, the duo appeared in all weekly meetings and stuff like that together. So obvious was their combined presence that all doctors in the health department of BMC had started thinking of Animesh as a cat's paw of Koutilya. An entomologist adorned with a degree of PhD became the pawn of a doctor.

In June 2010, a new political party won the corporation election and began to rule BMC. Jagannath Panja became the member of the mayor-in-council (Health). Entomologist Munda and Dr Nirjan Baker, the then borough executive health officer, became the official advisers to Jagannath Panja following the instructions of the city mayor, Gopiballabh Chatterjee.

Selection of Munda as an adviser was not accepted by the medical fraternity of BMC. Like other doctors of the department, Koutilya too became disappointed. Animesh became an unknown creature to him overnight. In the early 2013, Jagannath Panja made Munda the officer on special duty (OSD) and asked him to look after mosquito control activities for prevention and control of malaria and dengue in the city.

Mr Panja's decision was not accepted by the medical fraternity of BMC. Like his brethren, he too turned furious. Whispering campaign against the very entomologist began among the docs of the department. Putting their political identities aside, they stood united against Animesh and began teasing him in different ways. Munda's new-born dada too became class-conscious. He stopped talking to Munda. He stopped making phone calls to Munda. In a very strategic manner, his close friends began to spread this message among the doctors of the department that by labelling the tag of OSD (Health) on a nonmedical man, Jagannath Panja had insulted the entire medical fraternity and he would face the consequence soon. No doctor of BMC would work for him. Some of his friends said, "He is a doctor and he is more competent than Animesh and he can look after mosquito control activities better than him. To douse the resentment of BMC's doctors, Mr Panja should make the replacement immediately. Animesh cannot be the in-charge of mosquito control activities of BMC. Ward medical officers have been steering such activities in different wards of the corporation since long. A non-medical man cannot be the boss of doctors . . ."

However, the MMIC (Health) did not change his decision. He asked Animesh not to fall into the clutches of any blistering criticism about him. But this man was too weak to follow his advice. He could not run against the flow. And there was none to stand by him. Instead of helping the entomologist, the docs began demoralising him by playing various tricks. Koutilya too resorted to one together with Dr Bhootnath Batabyal, health coordinator, and Dr Nasir Hussain, deputy chief municipal health officer. Sitting right in front of the CMHO, Dr Nirjan Baker, the trio started bothering Munda in different ways. They used to fabricate complicated issues and place them before Munda for solution. They used to provoke the entomologist beyond his endurance.

Munda is a patient of fear psychosis. Hence he began to lose his temper against their mockery. His rhythm of life was lost. His sleep was disturbed. A fear of helplessness gripped his mind. He started feeling stressed and demoralised. His BP began to fluctuate every now and then. But nobody stood by him to share his tension. Nobody stood by him with an assurance of support. Issues not related to mosquito control started pouring in from different health units of BMC through CMHO. Official files relating to maternity homes, transfer of staff, engagement of contractual staff, bills for hired vehicles, which were supposed to be dealt with by deputy CMHOs, started coming to Munda from CMHO. Though Munda's duty as the OSD (Health) was to steer only the mosquito control programme of BMC, doctors of the department, including Dr Nirjan Baker, CMHO, started giving Munda the impression that he would have to look after other health related issues too as the OSD (Health). Munda made several requests to Dr Baker not to embarrass him by sending irrelevant files to him. But Dr Baker did not listen to him. A bit frustrated, Munda decided to part with the tag of OSD and he did it taking the consent of Mr Panja. And quite naturally, his enemies in disguise such as Dr Koutilya Makal, Dr Bhoothnath Batabyal, Dr Nasir Hussain and all other doctors of the department were highly elated with such decision of Munda.

Since January 2013, much water has flown down the River Ganga. For reasons best known to him, Koutilya has been out to humiliate Munda in different ways. In May

2013, Mr Panja asked Dr Baker to absorb him against the permanent post of a deputy CMHO. Dr Baker did it. Two-three days after giving the permanent portfolio of deputy CMHO to him, Mr Panja made him the OSD (Health) and asked him to look after mosquito control activities in different wards of BMC. But the doc was not happy with such assignment. He sought permission from Mr Panja to look after only the office of Animesh instead.

His intention was crystal-clear. He was not bothered about overseeing mosquito control activities of the department. All he wanted to do was just to humiliate the entomologist and compel him to work as a slave of his. He was aware that mosquito control operations in Beldanga were not running under the control of Munda. Medical officers (MOs) had been looking after the job since 1997 under the administrative control of borough executive health officers. The professional career of Animesh was religiously finished by the former CMHO of BMC, Dr Gourhari Ghosh. To protect the identities of MOs, Dr Ghosh performed the heinous crime of cribbing Munda most religiously. Officially, Munda had no right to interfere in the activities of an MO since Munda and an MO were of the same official rank.

The office of Animesh had nothing to do with the city's mosquito control activities. Officially, he is 'nobody' in the field of mosquito control activities of BMC. Jagannath Panja and Nirjan Baker, who considered themselves very intelligent, could not understand this very simple fact.

His dream came true. He became Munda's boss. His behaviour changed. By sending SMS, he began asking

Animesh to attend trivial meetings here and there despite the awareness that this very man remains badly busy doing many other face-saving job of the department following the instructions of the MMIC (Health) and CMHO.

The doc became more of a liability rather than a help to Munda. The sight of seeing Munda complying with his instructions was indeed very enchanting and this was bringing him a heavenly bliss everyday. His way of addressing Animesh too changed suddenly. He began calling him Dr Munda, instead of Animesh. In almost every weekly meeting of borough executive health officers held in the chamber of CMHO, he began to prove that he knew the subject of mosquito abatement much better than Munda. He started arguing with Munda and the other three entomologists of the department in an abrasive voice. Instead of improving the quality of mosquito control activities around the city, he started demoralising Munda and his colleagues. He was out to jeopardise mosquito control programme of BMC by way of misbehaving with Munda's team. Clearly, like many other docs of the department, he too was trying hard to botch up Mr Panja's dream project of mosquito control in the city of Beldanga. Strangely, Mr Panja was not aware of this, nor did anybody dare to bring this to his notice.

Instance two

On 10 June 2013, Dr Kamdev Kulkarni, borough executive health officer of BMC, sent an SMS to Munda. Munda received the SMS at 8.29 pm. The SMS read:

"You are requested to attend a meeting on prevention and control of mosquito-borne diseases. The meeting will be held tomorrow at 3 pm in the chamber of chief municipal health officer (CMHO)."

The day after, leaving all his important pre-scheduled official assignments unaccomplished, Munda rushed to the headquarters of BMC. He entered the chamber of CMHO, Dr Nirjan Baker, and asked him about the meeting. But no answer came from him. "Meeting?" Dr Baker frowned. "I don't know. Who has told you? Nobody has informed me yet."

A bit confused, Munda rang up Kamdev and asked, "Who has called today's meeting?"

"Makalda," Kamdev said. "Our CMHO has formed a core committee on mosquito control and Makalda has become the committee's chairman. Yesterday, while leaving the chamber of the MMIC (Health) at around 8 pm, Makalda told me to inform you and all other members of the core committee by SMSing."

"Ok. Got it." After disconnecting the line, Munda sat in the room of CMHO. Health coordinator, Bhootnath Batabyal, was searching on net using the computer of CMHO. Minutes later—Anath Ghosh, Gajapati Bhattacharya and Chotur Roychowdhury—all deputy CMHOs, came in and took their seats beside me, one after another.

"Where is our fourth deputy?" Gajapati asked Munda with a derisive smile.

"I don't know." Munda replied. "May be busy somewhere around . . ." Before he could finish, Nasir Hussain, fourth deputy CMHO, walked in. He talked to

CMHO for a little while and then, glancing sideways, left the room for the day.

At around 3.25 pm, Dr Koutilya Makal, deputy CMHO and OSD (Health), appeared from a nearby room carrying with him a thick register and then, sitting beside CMHO, said, "Convener of the core committee is coming. He's on the way." Having said this, he asked Gajapati if he could provide him a photocopy of the CMHO's communiqué concerning the formation of the core committee. Gajapati said "yes" to him. "You will get it."

Kamdev arrived at 4.15 pm with an ebony-skinned young boy carrying a huge bag in his back. The boy put the bag on the table of CMHO and disappeared.

Taking out a sheet of paper from his bag, Kamdev sat beside Makal, wrote down the names of the committee members and asked Makal, "Should I now start, Chairman-saheb?"

"Of course!" Makal shook his head. "You are the convener. Who else will do? Go ahead."

The meeting of the core committee started at 4.35 pm and it started with a query from Anath Ghosh. He asked, "What's the meaning of core committee? And what will be the functions of this committee?"

Makal explained, "It's a high-power committee. It will discuss about serious problems concerning mosquito-borne disease control activities of the department, find out means of solving them and then place its recommendations before the MMIC (Health) through CMHO for his adjudication. And then, after getting an endorsement from him, the borough executive health officers will be asked to implement the committee's recommendations in different wards of the city."

As Makal stopped, Anath asked, "What topic shall we discuss today?"

Before Makal could answer him, Bhootnath, member of the core committee, interjected. He said, "We need to discuss a very serious issue and it's all about the 100 days workers provided by different ward councillors under the state urban employment scheme. These workers have been working in tandem with the mosquito control staff of our ward health units (WHUs) since March this year. Unfortunately, they still do not know their working hours. Can't we fix up their duty-hours from 8 am to 2 pm, just at par with the duty hours of the staff of our WHUs . . . ?"

Having listened to the problem, Munda became disappointed. "All ridiculous bullshit!" he muttered to himself. "Is this an issue? They are already aware and all are working accordingly . . ."

Amid discussion, Sanjeev Das, attendant of CMHO, gave samosa and tea to CMHO, Makal and other officials present in the meeting. The focus of discussion was shifted at once. Makal and Batabyal started talking about the quality of samosa. The meeting ended at 5.30 pm with the announcement made by Dr Makal, "We will sit next week again and discuss many other important issues relating to mosquito control, etc."

Munda spent a long two-and-half hours listening to all those nonsense conversations. Not a single word regarding his subject, mosquito control, came up in the meeting for discussion.

And the CMHO was all along busy signing files and receiving phone calls . . .

Instance three

Prompt transport of a dengue virus across the country or from one country to another is very much possible if mosquitoes carrying such virus in their body get the chance of travelling in aircrafts. To prevent such transport, the airport authorities around the world always remain alert and take all possible measures for mosquito abatement in and around the airport areas on a regular basis.

How was the authority of Beldanga Airport doing the job? The Ministry of Health and Family Welfare, Government of India, wanted to get a comprehensive report of this from Dr Bakreshwar Sen, senior regional director of the regional office for Health & FW located in Sugar Lake Township in the eastern part of Beldanga City. Dr Sen was asked by the Central Ministry to send the report positively by 11 July 2013. To prepare such report, Dr Sen needed some information from fields and hence he planned to undertake an entomological survey at the airport area by detailing some staff from his office on 9 and 10 July 2013. But conducting such study only by the staff of Dr Sen seemed quite tough since he did not have any adept in entomology in his office. Finding no other alternative to resolve the crisis, Dr Sen wrote a letter to Dr Nirjan Baker on 25 June 2013, urging him to depute at least one entomologist at the airport of Beldanga on 9 and 10 July 2013 to help him run the surveillance quite smoothly. The survey, which was planned by Dr Sen, was indeed very important since it would help obtain precise information regarding the prevalence of breeding sources of dengue spreading mosquitoes—*Aedes aegypti* and *Aedes albopictus*—at the airport area. Dr Sen had no way to escape the directive.

Dr Nirjan Baker, CMHO, got Dr Sen's letter on 27 June 2013. As the controlling officer of the health department of BMC, Dr Baker was supposed to send the letter down to Munda with a clear instruction about the issue of detailing one entomologist from his department. Strangely, he did not do this. He sent the letter to Munda with this equivocal note: "Subject to approval of the Hon'ble MMIC (Health)."

The CMHO's note reached Munda 4 days later. It was 2 July 2013. Sitting in his office, 1.5 km away from the office of CMHO, Munda was writing an important report to be sent to his immediate official Boss, Dr Koutilya Makal. The letter of CMHO distracted Munda's focus. Secretion of adrenalin started getting pumped into his bloodstream.

"Subject to approval . . ." Munda read the line once, twice, thrice . . . and became terribly shocked since the note had come from none other than Nirjan Baker, a man for whom Munda had a special corner in his mind. "Nirjanda too is against me. By writing one line, he has killed my trust," Munda muttered to himself. "He is also out to abuse me. The man who I have respected for all these 14-15 years as my own elder brother and have always said "yes" to each and every instruction of his has finally proved that he's not a man of mine. Like all other doctors of BMC, he too is against an entomologist. How far is the room of our MMIC from his chamber? Nirjanda spends 2-3 hours with him everyday. He could have obtained his instruction quite easily. How can he, who has long been projecting himself as a well wisher of mine, make me waste my valuable time using such a dirty trick . . . ?"

Around 5 pm, putting his unfinished work at rest, Munda left for BMC headquarters to get to know the decision of Jagannath Panja, MMIC (Health). Half an hour later, he reached the chamber of CMHO. Sitting in his spacious AC room, he was chatting with his deputy CMHOs—Koutilya, Gajapati, Nasir, Chotur and Anath—vaccine administering officer Champa Choturbedi, dog sterilising officer Kripasindhu Kirtania and health coordinator Bhootnath Batabyal.

Munda went close to Nirjan and requested him to go with him to Mr Panja's chamber.

"Member has left for the day," Nirjan said, smile faced. "No problem, we will sort it out tomorrow . . ." Having said this, he stood up from his chair and left for home.

The next day (on 3 July) Munda again went to the headquarters of BMC, met Mr Panja together with Nirjan and got the MMIC's "yes" to Dr Sen's request for deployment of one entomologist from the end of BMC at the airport of Beldanga. A very small piece of work that Dr Baker could have done in a fraction of a minute compelled Munda to run to BMC headquarters on two subsequent days from his office. Munda now understands why people of Beldanga do not respect an employee of Beldanga Municipal Corporation.

Instance four

In a bid to step up mosquito control activities across the city of Beldanga, the health department of BMC constituted 15 Antimosquito Brigades in March 2013 by deploying 165 field workers (FWs) through an agency. The department took this initiative after getting a go-ahead from the mayor-in-council (MIC, in short) of BMC, the highest policy-making body of the corporation.

The proposal for deployment of 165 FWs against vacancies created in the department consequent upon promotion and retirement of many FWs had been initiated by the then deputy CMHO and OSD (Health) Dr Nirjan Baker on 15 March 2012. The proposal was then routed to the municipal commissioner through the chief municipal health officer, joint municipal commissioner and the member of the mayor-in-council (Health) of BMC. And finally, the approval was obtained from the MIC.

This was purely an administrative matter and Animesh Munda, entomologist, had nothing to do with this. Munda's role in this affair was only to take interview of candidates, choose the suitable candidates from them and impart training to the selected candidates on methodologies of mosquito control prior to their placement in different wards of BMC.

Issues concerning recruitment of staff, their transfer and promotion had never been the concern of Munda. Unfortunately, Munda still had no way to escape queries on these matters by the accounts department of BMC. One such incidence occurred very recently.

It was in the afternoon of 15 June 2013. Sitting in his office together with three consultant entomologists, Munda was doing analysis of data on distribution of breeding sites of the dengue spreading mosquito *Aedes aegypti* collected from different places in the southern part of the city over the past 1 year. He was doing a very serious job since the MMIC (Health), Jagannath Panja, had himself asked Munda to write a paper on *Aedes aegypti* explaining how the mosquito was changing its breeding habit in Beldanga.

Suddenly, there was a call.

"Chapalasundari calling," Munda saw the caller's name on the screen of his cellphone.

"Yes," Munda responded in promptness. "What can I do for you, Madam?"

"Nothing much. Only two clarifications I need from you at the moment."

"Clarifications?" Munda asked with a forced smile indicative of disappointment. "Of what . . . ?"

". . . Under what terms and conditions were those 165 FWs deployed by the health department through an agency?" Chapala said, sitting by the side of Dr Nirjan Baker, CMHO. "And from which budget code of BMC will their monthly wages be incurred?"

Munda's eyes flashed with anger. What he had failed to do all these years was beautifully done by him on that day. In an abrasive voice, Munda said, "I don't know, Chapala. Please ask Dr Koutilya Makal, deputy CMHO & OSD (Health). Currently, he is the officer incharge of our mosquito control office. I don't know who initiated the proposal. Why are you asking me? I can't help you. Sorry. Bye."

Chapala Chakladar is a very efficient accounts officer. Among the employees of BMC, she is a well-known figure. A short thin sprightly young woman in her late thirties, Chapala is modest, helpful and extraordinarily dynamic. She speaks well. She sings well. She behaves well. And she writes well. About 5-6 years ago, Munda was introduced to her by Dr Nirjan Baker. Since then Chapala had been part of Munda's family. Animesh Munda considered her as his own younger sister.

"Chapala too is now pretending to be unaware. Had she been a bit more intelligent, she could have understood how Animesh Munda is abused by the medical fraternity of BMC. Sitting in the headquarters, they initiate proposals concerning deployment of field workers and place them at different borough health offices themselves. Then they ask their borough executive health officers to route the monthly wage bills of field workers to the accounts department through the office of Munda. Since 2000, this has been going on. Monthly wage bills of field workers from different borough health offices come to Munda's office where one clerk scrutinises the bills, gets them signed by Animesh Munda and then sends the bills to the accounts department for final verification and disposal. Chapalasundari does not know that the official head of Munda's office has always been a deputy CMHO and Animesh Munda is not meant for looking after the deputy CMHO's administrative job. If the concerned deputy CMHO runs his official activities sitting at the headquarters of BMC, how will the staff of Munda's office keep track of proposals initiated by their boss? Did I prescribe deployment of those 165 Field Workers? No. Then why was she seeking those clarifications from me? Presence of my signature in the bills signifies only my witness that one clerk of my office has checked the bills and that does not imply my involvement in their deployment. Chapalasundari has killed my trust. I will never forgive her. I considered her a well-wisher of mine but she too has emerged as an enemy . . ." Munda became depressed and left for home leaving his serious job unaccomplished.

Instance five

21 June 2013. Sitting in the chamber of CMHO, Munda was drafting a reply for Jagannath Panja, MMIC (Health), to be given in the monthly meeting of BMC on 25 June 2013 with regard to three propositions brought in by a ward councillor of the BMC's opposition party (named Proletariat Protection Front of India) for prevention of malaria and dengue in the city of Beldanga. Suddenly, there appeared a young contractual field worker (FW) from a room adjacent to the chamber of CMHO. Munda had known him for a couple of months. The FW came near to Munda and put a slip on the table before him together with the photocopy of an authoritative approval concerning reengagement of 485 FWs with effect from 1 July 2012.

Munda stopped writing and picked up the papers from the table. The slip carried an instruction for him from his boss. And it read: "Please put up a draft-proposal for extension of the tenure of reengagement of 485 FWs for another one year as the validity of the current proposal will expire on 30 June 2013. Send me the connected file too along with the draft."

Munda's face blushed with anger. He said to himself, "Sitting in the room at a stone-throwing distance, you are sending your instructions to me by a messenger. Am I your PA? How dare you ask an entomologist to do such work! Who's the HOD? If you cannot steer the administrative activities, then why did you choose to become the boss of our department? Are you here only to sign the files prepared by Animesh? Dear doc, sorry, Munda won't help you win such dirty game. A little while ago, you were here. You could have told me about this. But you said nothing. You are deliberately insulting me. One day I will make you pay for it."

The murmuring over, Dr Munda wrote, "Sorry, I can't do this. The file is not with me."

After sending his reply, the entomologist went to a toilet, muttering to himself, "What the hell are you doing here sitting at the BMC headquarters? I didn't initiate the proposal. Your brethren did it. Remember, four clinching documents are lying with me. On 30 June 2009, deputy CMHO Dashanan Das proposed for one-year reengagement of 485 FWs from 1 July 2009. Proposal for renewal of the term of their reengagement with effect from 1 July 2010 too was initiated by him on 1 June 2010. Thereafter, Dr Nirjan Baker, the then deputy CMHO & OSD (Health) came into the picture. On 13 June 2011 and 7 June 2012, Nirjanda proposed for reengagement of these field workers from 1 July 2011 to 30 June 2012 and from 1 July 2012 to 30 June 2013 respectively. Bloody idiot, I am an entomologist and I am not a record supplier. Stop abusing me. Had I been from a rich family, I would have quit my job right now and left this Black Building forever . . ."

As Animesh came out from the toilet, Dr Nirjan Baker, now CMHO, called him by a gesture. "Listen."

He went near to him. Dr Baker gave him a photocopy of the previous year's approval and said, "Just copy it and change the date. It will be from 1 July 2013."

"Ok," Munda nodded, keeping the document in a file of his and then, sipping his fifth cup of the day, resumed his job.

On 29 June 2013, the entomologist handed over the draft-proposal to the CMHO, and he got the proposal signed by the boss of Munda's office. Interestingly, he signed the proposal without asking for the connected file.

Munda Spent Half an Hour with a Doctor's Ladder

In a malaria-prone ward of BMC (Beldanga Municipal Corporation), the procreation of the city's prime malaria spreading mosquito *Anopheles stephensi* in uncovered overhead water tanks (OHTs) of many houses and multistorey buildings had been going unchecked due to their absolute inaccessibility to the mosquito control squads of BMC. The concerned house-owners were least bothered about it. In spite of being repeatedly requested by the health personnel of BMC, those house-owners had not taken any measure to improve the situation.

On a humid summer morning in the late June of 2013, the ward medical officer, Dr Digbijay Ojha, wrote a letter to his borough executive health officer, Dr Binodini Tarkalankar, urging her to provide him at least one 10-ft long ladder on an urgent basis so that periodic inspection of all inaccessible OHTs in his ward could easily be made by his staff for mosquito larvae.

Binodini, who had already proved herself as one of the most indisciplined civic officials, forwarded Ojha's requisition to her boss Dr Anath Ghosh, deputy CMHO, with a request to help them get the ladder at an early date.

Anath, a branded non-performer in the health department of BMC, kept the letter with him for two days. The issue of buying a ladder was so tough for him that Anath could not resolve it singlehandedly. In fact, Ojha's ladder created two problems in his mind. And he could not work them out himself. Two days later, Anath passed the Ojha's buck into the court of Dr Nirjan Baker, chief municipal health officer (CMHO), seeking his help in understanding two serious questions. One is, how a 10-ft ladder can be procured urgently. And the other is, if one field worker falls from the ladder, what will happen? The senior-most health officer, who is going to retire by the end of 2013, was pretending to be unable to solve this petty issue. How shocking!

Critics say that the health administration of BMC is very slow and quite unfriendly. Movement of files from one table to another is very slow. Most doctors of the department are erratic. They pretend to be very serious about their duties but aren't. There are five deputy CMHOs in the department to assist CMHO. But they do not do this. They are deceptive. They are back-stabbers. They remain busy waging a cold war against one another. Most of the times, they remain busy doing the things that serve only their own interests. They know how to escape their duties and responsibilities. And they're well conversant with the art of cashing in on services rendered by Animesh Munda and other juniors.

Queries of Ghosh reached Baker's table 3 days later.

Nirjan is a modest and proactive officer. Some higher officials of BMC consider him as the asset of the corporation. And, of course, he knows better who to hypnotise, when to hypnotise and how to hypnotise to fulfill his own interests.

Strangely, like Binodini and Anath, Nirjan too could not solve the ladder-problem of Ojha himself. Apprehending that the OSD (Health) wouldn't help him sort out the issue, Nirjan passed the buck into the court of Animesh Munda, entomologist, asking him to opine.

Munda turned furious. After all it was a case of ladder. Someone needs this to climb up to the top. Policy-decision has to be taken to resolve the riddle created by Ojha's ladder. What the hell would Munda do with the ladder-issue?

Munda, a non-medical doctorate, is hyperactive, ill-tempered and a chronic patient of fear-psychosis. Everyone can abuse him. Everyone can humiliate him. Everyone can lambaste him. Everyone can make him work like a slave. Truly speaking, I have never come across such an awesome idiot in my life ever before. Sitting on a very old armless wooden chair in a small abandoned room of BMC, the bastard Munda has been striving to comply with the instructions of his bosses with clockwork efficiency for the past 24 years without getting any recognition and promotion. Since he writes quite well, the health authority of BMC has made him work as a mere draftsman. Munda has never been allowed to accomplish tasks that an entomologist is supposed to do for the city of Beldanga.

A sense of hatred for the entire medical fraternity of BMC gripped his mind. His pox-scarred face welled up with contempt and anger. He wrote to Nirjan: "My opinion regarding question No 1 is, I do not know. My opinion about question No 2 is, I do not know . . ."

It took nearly half an hour for Munda to pacify his anger triggered by the irresponsible activities of Dr Baker and other doctors of BMC concerning one petty ladder.

No other person knew the activities of the health officials of BMC better than Munda. The man who Munda had long been respecting as his friend-philosopher-and-guide too finally came out to ridicule him. Munda had no other way to retaliate the humiliation than digesting it in utter silence. Munda had lost faith in the medical fraternity of BMC long before Munda unmasked Dr Nirjan Baker on that day. Munda's only lamentation was that he had spent a staggering 10-15 years unnecessarily boasting about Nirjan.

The countdown for Munda has begun. And, yes, he will leave the stuffy Black Building of BMC that day with tearful eyes, leaving his last departure unnoticed to all around.

Is Munda the man to visit burning ghats???

People's complaints of air pollution due to improper functioning of the pollution control devices (PCDs) at some burning ghats of BMC (Beldanga Municipal Corporation) were pouring in to his office for some days past. On 29 March 2012, Jagannath Panja, member of the mayor-in-council (Health) of BMC, made a surprise visit to one well-known burning ghat in the northern part of the city of Beldanga and experienced the problem himself.

After inspection, Mr Panja came to his office and called up Dr Nirjan Baker, the then deputy chief municipal health officer (Dy CMHO) and OSD (Health).

Nirjan Baker, the go-to-man of Jagannath Panja, appeared before him in a jiffy.

With a tinge of disgust in his voice, Mr Panja said, "The PCDs at our burning ghats are not working. Situation is horrible. Do form a monitoring committee within 24 hours and make Kripasindhu Kirtania (dog sterilising officer), the convener of the committee. The chief executive officer (CEO) of our electrical and engineering department is doing practically nothing with regard to the maintenance of PCDs . . ."

"Ok," Nirjan shook his head in agreement and then, after blinking his eyes for a brief while, constituted the committee involving two Dy CMHOs—Dr Koutilya Makal and Dr Nasir Hussain—and Animesh Munda, entomologist, as members of the committee and Kripasindhu Kirtania as the convener. Nirjan read out the names to Mr Panja and asked, "What will be the function of this committee, Sir?"

Mr Panja thought for a while and said, "The committee will critically look into the functioning of PCDs, interact with the staff of our burning ghats and local residents as to the performances of such devices. The committee will write to the concerned CEO seeking information from him regarding the contractors deployed by the CEO for doing maintenance of PCDs, cost of maintenance, period of contract, terms and conditions for their engagement, etc. The committee will write to the CEO seeking his cooperation with regard to issues relating to PCDs."

On 30 March 2013, by issuing a circular, Dr Dashanan Das, chief municipal health officer, intimated all concerned about the formation of the committee.

"When shall I go to Burning Ghat? Is performing such job possible for an entomologist? When shall I do my own work? Why is the man, who I have been respecting for long as the most dynamic and practical administrator, too now out to abuse me like the doctors of his department? Has Nirjanda trapped me in any way?" Munda muttered this to himself after seeing his name in the list of the members of the PCD monitoring committee.

More than a year has passed. Munda has not visited any burning ghat of BMC yet, nor has the convener of the committee, Mr Kirtania, ever asked him to attend any meeting on PCD. Are the PCDs now functioning properly? Is the committee functioning properly? Munda does not know. He only says, "The convener must have forgotten my name. Otherwise, a tainted officer of BMC in his late fifties, Kripasindhuda would have compelled me to waste my time attending a series of meetings on PCDs. Thank God, I have been saved from being abused by another crooked fellow of BMC . . ."

MUNDA'S SLIP OF TONGUE

It was late in the summer morning of a Sunday. Sitting beside the window of his small drawing-cum-dining room, Dr Animesh Munda, entomologist of BMC (Beldanga Municipal Corporation), was silently reading a book titled "THE OBAMAS" authored by Jodi Kantor.

Suddenly, the doorbell rang.

Sujata, Munda's wife, opened the door.

A robust young reporter of The Times of India—Aniket Roy—came in, smile-faced.

"What's happened, Aniket? Suddenly dropped in on me?" Munda said, closing the book.

"Boss has asked me to write a story," Aniket said, sitting on a chair beside Munda. "I need some inputs."

"Hmm," Munda shook his head with a cryptic smile. "Go ahead."

Sujata gave them tea and some biscuits.

Having sipped from his cup, Aniket asked, "What about dengue?"

"The situation is terrible!" Munda replied, taking out a medical journal (Public Health, volume 24, May 2013). "It's spreading very fast. As many as 134 countries are endemic. Over 3000 million people are at risk. Around 0.5 million patients of severe dengue (termed DHF), mostly children, are treated in hospitals each year and thousands of these patients die. Fifty to 100 million people suffer every year. According to Simon Hay of Oxford University, even 400 million cases of dengue might be realistic. The worldwide incidence of dengue has increased roughly 30-fold over the last five decades. The burden of dengue is huge. What we see is only the tip of an iceberg. I don't know what's going to happen around the world in the next 4-5 years . . ."

Noting down the figures, Aniket asked, "What is the WHO doing? Is it sleeping?"

"No," Munda pleaded. "The World Health Organization is now very much concerned about dengue. In its recent publication titled "Global Strategy for Dengue Prevention and Control, 2012-2020", the WHO has set out its specific goals to reduce mortality of dengue by at least 50% and its morbidity by at least 25% by 2020 (using 2010 as the baseline). Huge task! And to achieve this, we have to get three things done most religiously.

"First of all we need to improve the disease surveillance system to estimate the actual burden of the disease, since the true scale and distribution of dengue is still unclear. The second task is case management. And the third one is sustainable mosquito control . . ."

As Munda stopped, the reporter enquired, "What about dengue-vaccine? Without vaccine, we can't prevent dengue. Isn't it, Animeshda?"

Munda turned serious. "Wrong. You are absolutely wrong. Vaccine cannot help us win the fight against dengue," he said with a tinge of disgust in his voice. "We have vaccine against yellow fever. People still die. India produces vaccine against Japanese encephalitis (JE, in short) at its own vaccine producing unit in Himachal Pradesh. JE still breaks out in this country, killing the poor people in greater numbers. So, don't put so much of trust in vaccine. Without mosquito control, you cannot get rid of dengue, got my point? Currently, at least 9 candidate vaccines are in development. But the challenge is that a successful vaccine must protect against all four strains of dengue virus (DENV-1 to DENV-4). All said and done, it will take a number of years before it is known whether a vaccine is really effective. Even then, mosquito control will continue to play a vital role in reducing transmission rates to allow successful vaccine coverage. This is not my opinion, Aniket. The Associate Director of Science of the US Centres for Disease Control and Prevention, Ronald Rosenberg, has said this. You cannot ignore his views," Munda stopped at the interruption caused by Aniket.

"Are you against vaccine?" Aniket asked.

"No, no, I'm not," Munda replied, looking stern. "Vaccine is useful. There's no doubt about it. But you can use this as an additional tool to fight against dengue. Vaccine is not the permanent solution. Vaccination programme is very expensive. If you want to win the fight using a vaccine, you will have to vaccinate each and every individual in a dengue-prone area. But the task is monumental. Just think of the quantum of investment you will require for implementing such programme. In a country like India, given the threadbare infrastructure and the financial constraints, how will you undertake such a mammoth job, Aniket? It's not possible. Remember, when a successful vaccine becomes available in the near future, this will provide added impetus to mosquito control. As transmission rates start to fall, mosquito control will become more effective, as well as essential for preventing new outbreaks of the disease. Mosquito control will continue to remain the only path to reach the destiny. But that too is not possible in this country. Where is entomologist? Without entomologists, mosquito control is not possible. Doctors can't do this. They know very little about mosquitoes. Look at the doctors of BMC. They are looking after mosquito control activities around the city of Beldanga but they cannot identify a mosquito larva. They are not at all serious about the job. They cannot detect a mosquito breeding source in fields. Since 1997, they have been wasting public money in the name of supervising mosquito-bashing programme around the city," Munda stopped here, remained silent for some time looking still at his ant-eaten portrait hanging on the unclean wall before him. Then wiping his glasses with a handkerchief, he began, "As the chief municipal health officer, he could have introduced the system quite easily. The Marxist mayor of BMC was very close to him. But he did not discuss the issue with him. I needed just three entomologists to look after mosquito control programme across the city in a scientific way . . ."

"Animeshda," Aniket interjected. "Did you send any proposal to him?"

"Of course, I did," Munda burst out with anger. "But that conceited and bumptious Gourhari rebuffed my proposition outright."

Having said this, Munda took out a sheet of paper from an old file kept in an almirah at a corner of his room. "Yes, here's the thing," he resumed, showing the note to Aniket. "Look. I sent him the proposal for creating three posts of entomologists on 26 December 1997. On 9 January 1998, that idiot Dr Gourhari Ghosh wrote, 'Every borough of BMC has been provided with a health supervisor. What are the justifications for additional three entomologists? Is a borough executive health officer not competent enough?"

After reading the note of Gourhari, Munda said, "In 1997, Dr Gourhari Ghosh deployed doctors in different wards of BMC @ 1 doctor per ward and by issuing an official order, he asked them to steer mosquito control activities in the city. What the hell are those doctors doing? They are doing nothing. There are now 148 medical officers in the health department of BMC. 115 of them are contractual and the rest 33 are permanent. Contractually engaged doctors draw rupees 35 thousand each per month. The permanent doctors draw 50-80 thousand each per month. Some MOs, especially those who are placed at the 28 charitable dispensaries of BMC, are quite good. They spend 3-4 hours everyday doing medical check-ups for poor patients. Among the others, some 10-15 MOs are quite serious. They do some work for the department and draw their salaries. But the others are worthless. They come to office late and leave early. To them, offices are nothing but retiring rooms.

"There's no specific job for them. Sitting in offices, they spend time talking all nonsense to their subordinates. The health department of BMC runs an immunisation programme once a week in each ward of the city, but this work is looked after mainly by some trained honorary health workers, no matter whether an MO is present or not in the ward office. At the clinics of BMC, blood tests for malaria, dengue and platelet count are all done by trained laboratory technicians and they distribute the medicines themselves among the patients of malaria, following the guidelines of the directorate of NVBDCP (National Vector Borne Disease Control Programme), Government of India. Presence of an MO at a malaria clinic of BMC is not mandatory, Aniket. Laboratory technicians are competent enough.

"As far as mosquito control is concerned, there too, MOs play no role. They do not know how to identify a mosquito larva. They do not visit fields to check activities of their mosquito control staff. They do not know how to implement the national guidelines for mosquito control. I have given them training on mosquito control several times. Still they have learned nothing. They are very reluctant and casual about mosquito control. But they are very lucky guys. All are in safe hands of our political dadas. Nobody can finger them. Nobody can touch them. Some of them have of late put on green jerseys, showing their loyalty to the political party now in power in BMC as well as in the state of Jhautala, while some have still clung on to their former colour—the red. Contrarily, I don't have any political back-up. I am a soft target. The controlling officials of the health department of BMC use me as a shuttle-cock. Anyone can humiliate me. Anyone can abuse me." Munda stopped here for some while, had a glass of water and then, taking the day's sixth roll of betel-leaf, continued, "After coming to their offices, most of the ward MOs spend their times attending phone calls from their patients, friends and family members. They do nothing for BMC."

"Really?" Aniket asked, utterly confused. "I think you are going wrong. Can a doctor spend the day sitting idle? I don't believe this. It's sheer crap. As far as I know, they do a lot for BMC."

"Who said this?" Munda asked scornfully. "Listen. On 3 July 2013, sitting in the chamber of Dr Nirjan Baker, chief municipal health officer, I simply asked our deputy CMHO & OSD (Health) Dr Kolutilya Makal about the daily activities of an MO. Dr Makal turned furious. He rudely asked me to download the information from the website of BMC. And he told this despite the awareness that no such information is available in that website.

"Dr Bhootnath Batabyal, health coordinator, too was present in the CMHO's chamber at that point of time. He was brushing up some reports sitting beside me. I asked him the same question. Bhootnath looked at me sternly. I asked him the question again. Initially, he stuttered for some while and then, suddenly began to lambaste me, 'Stop drilling the MOs. Why are you running after them? It's very bad.' That day I first realised the deep-rooted love of a doctor for another doctor. And that day I first noticed a clear line of barrier between an entomologist and a doctor in the health department of BMC . . ."

"But," Aniket interrupted. "Mr Panja told me some other story that day about the MOs. He said . . ."

"I know, I know," Munda snapped. "The MMIC (Health) told you that following his instructions, the ward MOs of BMC had been sincerely checking health conditions of poor patients and providing medicines to them from their offices for treatment of common ailments such as fever, fungal infection, gastroenteritis, allergies, cough and cold, urinary tract infection, etc. Right? And you got an impression that the MOs of our department were really serving the poor. Isn't it?"

"Yes," Aniket nodded. "Aren't they doing a lot for the society?"

"Fuck all!" Munda retorted wryly. "Listen. How many patients do visit a ward health unit per day? Note down the figures. Somewhere it's zero. Somewhere it's 1-2. And somewhere it's 3-5. The number of ward offices recording daily attendance of 25-50 patients is just 4 or five.

"Our MMIC (Health) has also asked them to cause to collect names of malaria and dengue patients from the local practitioners, nursing homes and private pathological laboratories so that necessary mosquito control measures for preventing transmission of these diseases can be undertaken in and around the houses of the victims in promptness. How many of them are following the instructions of our MMIC? Hardly five or six. You cannot make them work. They are doctors. They are not scared of Jagannath Panja. If he goes against them, he will be in trouble. His own partymen will go against him. Remember this. Willy-nilly, Jagannath Panja has done another great favour for the ward MOs of BMC. He has assigned the job of monitoring mosquito control activities in a ward to an efficient non-medical staff working under the ward MO. His order has come to them as a tremendous boon. They are now flying as free birds. They come to office at their own will, record their attendance and draw their monthly remuneration. Getting lucrative salary without rendering any service is great! Dr Gourhari Ghosh has ruined Beldanga and the history will not forgive him. One day the political leaders of Beldanga will certainly realise this."

As Munda stopped, Aniket asked curiously, "Can't you monitor mosquito control activities in different wards of BMC yourself?"

"No. I can't. My official rank and the rank of an MO are same. In fact, I am nobody in the health department of BMC. Mosquito control workers and all other employees of ward health units are working under the administrative control of ward MOs. There are 15 borough executive health officers and they are placed in ranks above that of mine. They are my seniors. There are 5 deputy chief municipal health officers and they are seniors to borough executive health officers. The medical officers of our health department are my colleagues and they are not my subordinates. Where do I stand, Aniketbabu?"

As Munda stopped, Aniket asked, "Did you ever discuss your problem with Nishikantada?"

"Shit!" Munda sneered. "Don't utter the name of that old haggard. I just can't tolerate him. I had never seen such a worthless man ever before. I first met him in 1989. For two terms—from 1985 to 1990 and 2005 to 2010—he was our MMIC. But I still don't know what he had exactly done for the department. He was a carbon copy of Dr Gourhari Ghosh. He was too cunning and too shrewd."

"Did you discuss the issue with him?" Aniket asked.

"Yes, I did, in the early 2006," Munda replied in a dismal voice. "But he turned it down, saying that the department would have to forgo three permanent posts to create three posts of entomologists. He commented this being suggested by a highly corrupt doctor of the department, Dr Ritabrata Bose. As an alternative option, I also urged him to deploy three entomologists on a contractual basis. But that too was rebuffed. Like Dr Gourhari Ghosh, Dr Nishikanta Dey too was deadly against deployment of any entomologist in the department. Dr Dey had insulted me twice during 2005-2010, for no faults of mine at the provocation of Dr Ritabrata Bose and Dr Dashanan Das. I will never forget those days of humiliation. I wish I could have butchered him and pumped all bullets of a gun into his chest. And I will be the happiest man if that rascal dies an awful death in a road accident."

Despite the thought that it might displease him, Aniket said, "Truly speaking, BMC is not the right place for an entomologist having a degree of PhD. Why didn't you try for an independent research-oriented job someplace else?"

After a brief silence, Munda said, "No. I could not do that. I had some problems . . ."

Sujata gave another cup of tea to Aniket. He finished his cup briskly and left, saying, "You'll find the story in tomorrow's edition. Bye . . ."

Munda's concern about JE

Producing rice apart, a paddy field produces mosquitoes too, some of which are very dangerous because they spread Japanese encephalitis (JE), the deadliest of all insect-borne diseases. Caused by a virus, JE occurs mainly in China, East Indies, Republic of Korea, Indonesia, Thailand, Guam, Taiwan, Philippines, Myanmar, Bangladesh and India. Strangely, JE has unveiled its gruesome face in Siberia too, the northeast part of the USSR which remains covered with ice more than half the year. The rural populations that live in huts close to paddy fields and rear pigs mainly suffer from this malady.

JE is a very dangerous disease. Within 24 hours following the infection of the JE-virus, the three-layered shield of the brain gets severely affected. As a result, patients develop high fever and some life-threatening symptoms such as intense headache, nausea and vomiting, abnormal movements, incoherent speech, seizures and finally a state of unconsciousness. Since there is no specific treatment for JE, 20 to 50% of the patients die, and the death occurs normally within 10 days after the infection. Those who somehow survive the onslaught, save for a very few cases, continue to live with an incurable aberration such as mental impairment, loss of memory or severe neurological instability. Some of the survivors even become paralysed and remain so for the rest of the life.

There are twenty-seven types of mosquitoes around the world that spread JE. In India, the disease is transmitted mainly by three types of mosquitoes and these are: *Culex vishnui*, *Culex pseudovishnui* and *Culex tritaeniorhynchus*.

JE is basically a zoonotic disease (ailment of animals) and pigs are the prime amplifying hosts of its virus. Apart from pigs, bats and some species of birds such as pond herons (*Ardeola grayii*) and cattle egrets (*Bubulcus ibis*) also play their part in maintaining the natural circulation of JE-virus. People are merely incidental victims and such incident occurs especially when both the populations of the JE-bearing mosquitoes and the load of the JE-virus increase simultaneously in nature. JE never spreads from a man to another man.

Mosquitoes that spread JE are primarily zoophilic. They prefer cattle's blood more than the blood of birds, pigs and other animals. Man becomes their diet when their populations in the environment increase or in case they miss their preferred host or in situations where people sleep in cattlesheds, unprotected.

To get a drop of blood, the JE-bearing mosquitoes bite from sunset to sunrise. After taking blood-meals, they take rest for two to three days. And they take rest sitting in the dark, moist corners of cattlesheds, piggeries and human-dwellings. Spawning starts thereafter. These mosquitoes lay their eggs in paddy fields, wells, ponds, ditches, puddles, ground-pools, burrow-pits and other such places. However, their main breeding-ground is a paddy field. Given the nature of their breeding sites, destroying these mosquitoes at source by spraying larvicides or any other measure is very tough.

There is no specific treatment for JE. The most effective way of preventing an outbreak of this dreaded disease is vaccination. Japan has shown that vaccination works wonders. To successfully implement the vaccination programme, we first need to pinpoint the people in peril and then vaccinate them at random. Initially, two doses of vaccine—1 ml each (0.5 ml for children below 3)—have to be administered at an interval of 7-14 days and then a booster dose be given within one year to make people completely immune to the JE-virus. But one needs to remember that the task of vaccinating people has to be accomplished always before the onset of the season of JE-outbreak because, like other vaccines, the JE vaccine too doesn't play any role in terminating an outbreak.

Is carrying out such a vaccination programme tough in India? No. The country has its own JE vaccine-producing machinery in Kasauli, named Central Research Institute (CRI). The vaccine produced by the CRI is safe and highly effective. Most importantly, the CRI has a capacity to produce as much vaccine as required by different states of the country. Unfortunately, demands for the vaccine from different JE-prone states usually reach the Central government only when the disease breaks out.

To prevent mosquito-bites, insecticide-treated mosquito nets (ITNs) are more protective than ordinary mosquito nets. Hence people living in JE-prone areas ought to use ITNs.

Some people sleep inside piggeries and cattlesheds for preventing theft of pigs and cattle. Such practice is dangerous because it makes people more exposed to the infective bites. So it has to be stopped.

Dr Munda's concern about JE is that a national programme for preventing transmission of JE has not been launched yet in India, nor has any budgetary provision been made to wage a battle against this killer disease. India has its own JE-vaccine producing machinery, but people here still die of JE. When will the political leaders of India seriously look into this serious public health problem?

Doctors'
Dereliction

It was a rain-clad evening on 28 July 2013. Sitting beside the Hon'ble Chief Minister of Jhautala at her residence in South Beldanga, Jagannath Panja, MMIC (Health) of BMC (Beldanga Municipal Corporation), boasted, "In the backdrop of the last year's episode of dengue in some areas of the city, we have undertaken several measures to prevent its outbreak this year. Our department has been working religiously from the beginning of the year at your behest, Didi . . ."

"Mr Panja," CM interrupted, "What about your ward MOs (medical officers)? Are they sincere?"

"Yes, Didi," Mr Panja replied with a beatific smile. "Our MOs are very honest and they are now working very sincerely. The previous board of BMC did not use them properly. Rather it had abused them. After coming to office, they used to run only after mosquitoes. Theirs was a wretched life at that time. The Proletariat Protection Front of India did not have any plan to use them for our society. I have changed the system. At your behest, I asked them to concentrate more on the clinical aspects of dengue and malaria and they have been doing their job meticulously right from March 2013. Every ward MO is an asset of our corporation. They are damn nice. Clad in green jerseys, they are now looking very smart and handsome. The old laggards too have become rejuvenated. A new era of activities has ushered in! Besides, one efficient officer, named Dr Koutilya Makal, is now directly overseeing our mosquito control activities. Dr Makal is a very aggressive officer and everyone fears him. I am proud of him, Didi . . ."

As Jagannath Panja stopped, the CM asked him with a frown of disappointment, "Come to the point, Jagannath. I have no time to listen to who's doing what in BMC. Do just answer me, yes or no. Are your ward medical officers collecting dengue and malaria-related information from their local practising physicians on a daily basis?"

Apprehending that his answer might displease the CM, Mr Panja began to stutter, "Y-yes, I mean, they s-sometimes . . ."

"Ok, ok," the CM snapped. "I know what they are doing. Changing jerseys does not mean that they have become loyal to BMC. Send them back to their old pavilion. A rotten lot! Many of them are deliberately committing sabotage. Don't you realise this? You are an intelligent leader of our party. First identify your enemies. Otherwise you will be in trouble. They are not following your instructions. Be careful! By the way, do you know Dr Asim Batra? His chamber is just opposite the Beldanga Technical Institute . . . It's very near to your Black Building. Dr Batra is a very good doctor and he's loyal to our party. Yesterday I got one message from him. It's terrible!" Having said this, the CM opened the inbox of her cellphone and showed Dr Batra's SMS to Jagannath Panja.

The SMS read: "Madam, after 2-3 years, I am now coming across some cases of malaria. This is not a good sign, regards, etc."

After reading the message, Mr Panja's face turned pale. "L-let me check it, Didi." Saying this, Mr Panja left the residence of the CM, grim-faced.

At around 8 pm, while coming back home, Mr Panja called up Dr Nirjan Baker, chief municipal health officer of BMC, and told him all that he had heard from the CM and snubbed, "Dr Baker, what are you doing? Am I there to look after each and every petty issue of the department? What the hell are you and your team doing? I need information from Dr Asim Batra within 24 hours."

Dr Nirjan Baker was obviously getting embarrassed by the verbal onslaught of Jagannath Panja but he had no way to escape the attack. The conversation over, Dr Baker phoned Dr Animesh Munda, entomologist, and asked him to collect the names and addresses of all malaria patients from the clinic of Dr Batra on an urgent basis.

"Ok. I'll do it tomorrow morning," Munda assured him, adding, "Nirjanda, don't spare the ward MO. Dr Batra's chamber is just 2-3 minutes from his ward health unit. What has he done all these days sitting in the office? He could have collected the information quite easily. Nirjanda, your MOs are out to tarnish your image. Like our MMIC (Health), you too have repeatedly been asking them to collect reports on malaria/dengue from nursing homes, private pathological laboratories, local medical practitioners and all other such non-KMC sources on a regular basis. But, I am sorry to say, most of them are not doing the job. They are deliberately violating your instructions. Please take them to task immediately. Don't trust them. They are out to jeopardise our programme."

No response came from the other end. Before disconnecting the line, the timid voice only said, "One information from Ward No. 143 has just reached me from the cellphone of our Hon'ble Member. It's about the hospitalisation of a school student. His blood-test has proved positive for dengue . . . What the hell is our great Makal doing now? Like the MO of that ward, he too is now sleeping. Let them sleep. Goodnight."

Panja's pride pricked by a doctor

Reports concerning recurrent breeding of both malaria and dengue spreading mosquitoes in the premises of Beldanga Medical College and Hospital (BMC&H) had long been pouring in to his office from the concerned officials of his department. Visibly disappointed, Jagannath Panja, member of the mayor-in-council (Health) of BMC (Beldanga Municipal Corporation), made a surprise visit to the medical college on 12 June 2013 accompanied by some health officials and one antimosquito brigade.

Mr Panja spent nearly one hour making thorough inspection of the hospital premises together with his team. Rainwater-filled bitumen drums, clogged open surface drains, uncovered water reservoirs, small plastic cups and other discarded items lying strewn over here and there and some other water-holding sites harbouring mosquito larvae in greater numbers came to his notice.

The inspection over, Mr Panja made a press-brief standing under the biting sun and then, he entered the chamber of the principal of the BMC&H, Dr Kalikrishna Lahiri. The hospital superintendent, concerned engineer of the public welfare department and some other officials from the end of the BMC&H too participated in the meeting. Mr Panja shared with them his observation regarding mosquitogenic conditions prevailing within the campus of the medical college and urged the principal to take some corrective measures to improve the situation on an urgent basis.

During the course of discussion, Mr Panja requested the principal to ask his students, studying preventive and social medicine, to visit the college premises at least for half an hour at weekly intervals to have a practical experience of identifying mosquito larvae in fields. That such in-field training would help the medical students become efficient public health professionals in future was also pointed out by Mr Panja. After minutely listening to him, Dr Lahiri assured Mr Panja that he would certainly implement his proposition for the benefit of the city.

"Keep the medical college under scanner," having given this instruction to his officials, Mr Panja left the BMC&H with a self-gratifying smile across his glossy face.

The concept of detecting and destroying mosquito breeding sites in the premises of medical colleges and hospitals by mobilising students of the same medical colleges was new and it was the brainchild of Jagannath Panja. After having propounded this, Mr Panja's chest puffed up with pride. To implement this, he asked Dr Nirjan Baker, chief municipal health officer of BMC, to write a letter of request to the principals of all medical colleges located in the city of Beldanga, including Dr Kalikrishna Lahiri.

Dr Nirjan Baker did the job on 14 June 2013. The letter he wrote, read: "Dear Sir, the monsoon has set in and with this, the city's environmental conduciveness to the procreation of *Aedes aegypti*, *Anopheles stephensi* and other types of mosquitoes has begun increasing. As you are well aware, the prime dengue-bearing species *Aedes aegypti* is basically a small container breeder and hence, following the accumulation of rainwater here and there, like many other places around the city of Beldanga, the premises of your esteemed medical college and hospital, we apprehend, too, will help these mosquitoes breed quite easily in case small plastic containers, biomedical wastes, tyres, abandoned bitumen drums, bottles, coconut shells, earthen pots, accumulation of rainwater in any low-lying place; accumulation of seepage water on rooftops of the buildings of your college, hospital and students' hostel remain unnoticed. After discussing this issue with our experts, we have sorted out a plan which you may please implement on an urgent basis. The plan is: If your faculty members of the department of preventive and social medicine ask their MBBS students to consider the premises of your medical college and hospital a big laboratory and make a search just once a week for detection and destruction of mosquito breeding sources by applying some common-sense approaches (without using any insecticide), their initiative will work wonders. If you need our help in terms of providing any training to your faculty members for identification of mosquito larvae, please feel free to talk to us. We will do.

"And last but not the least, as a man of the medical fraternity, I am hopeful that if our beloved students of

MBBS are given the scope of identifying mosquito larvae during the period of their studies, their interest about this subject will grow and that will help them deliver their service in a better way in future in case they opt public health as their career option, etc."

One week later, antimosquito brigade of BMC, led by Mohini Biswas, consultant entomologist, made a follow-up visit to the premises of BMC&H as per the instructions of Mr Panja. But the BMC team came back depressed. No sign of improvement came to their notice. Dr Kalikrishna Lahiri was indeed too busy to recall what he had promised to Mr Panja on 12 June.

Truly, it's incredible India!!!

Munda's leaflet
messed up by doctors

It was in the late May of 2013. Sitting alone in his chamber, Jagannath Panja, member of the mayor-in-council (Health) of BMC (Beldanga Municipal Corporation), had been talking to his PA on a grave official matter. Suddenly, a leader of the Proletariat Protection Front of India (PPFI), named Dhananjoy Chakraborty, walked in briskly, delivered a letter to Mr Panja in an envelope and left his chamber after a brief chat with him.

Mr Panja took out the letter and read, "Dear Sir, two species of mosquitoes in the city of Beldanga are our enemies—*Anopheles stephensi* and *Aedes aegypti*. The first one spreads malaria, the second one spreads dengue and chikungunya. Both of them breed mostly in clean water collections. Their larvae are commonly found in domestic water storage containers in and around human-dwellings. And the water storage practice among our city-dwellers is the main reason why the larvae of these two mosquitoes occur in domestic water containers almost round the year.

"In my constituency, people are modest but very poor. They live in slums where water supply is inadequate. Hence they store water, paving the way for mosquito procreation throughout the year. But my voters are helpless. They can't change their habit. Give them adequate water first and then ask them to follow your instructions.

"Yesterday, some mosquito control workers from your health department made a blunder. They visited some slums in my area and detected mosquito larvae in drums, masonry tanks and earthen pitchers. After detection, they asked my people to destroy mosquito larvae by throwing away the water from their water containers. After hearing this, some of my voters became angry and started breathing fire at them. This created a big problem. Had I reached there a bit late, your staff would have been beaten up by my voters. Please ask your mosquito control staff to stop visiting our slums. Without providing adequate water supply, don't ask our slumdwellers to throw away water. They will not listen to you. Problem of water in my area is severe. The problem has to be solved on a war-footing. And I need your personal help to get it done . . . Yours faithfully, Dhananjoy Chakraborty."

Having read the letter of the leader of the PPFI, Mr Panja called up Dr Animesh Munda, entomologist of BMC, showed him the letter and asked him to bring out a leaflet containing some practicable tips for the slumdwellers of Beldanga, by applying which they could prevent mosquito breeding in their water storage containers themselves without wasting water any more.

Munda prepared the write-up overnight. He then gave it to Dr Nirjan Baker, chief municipal health officer (CMHO), for printing. And Dr Baker did it.

Twenty-five thousand copies of the leaflet were printed by the press of BMC in 48 hours. The leaflet contained these messages: 1. Collect guppy fish from your nearby ward health unit of BMC and release it in your masonry tanks, wells and other such big water reservoirs. This fish is a voracious feeder of mosquito larvae. 2. To kill mosquito larvae in earthen vats, pitchers, buckets, tin cans and other such containers, strain off the water using a thin cloth. Mosquito larvae thus isolated from water will die subsequently. 3. Wrap your water storage drums (plastic/iron) in a plastic sheet every night. Done, this will benefit you in four ways. A. Your water will be saved. B. Mosquitoes will not be able to enter the drums for laying eggs. C. In case adult mosquitoes emerge from pupae inside the drums, they will remain stranded therein and die of asphyxia. D. Since the plastic sheet is impervious to air, mosquito larvae wriggling inside the drums will not get sufficient oxygen, as a result of which some of them will die.

This was indeed a first-of-its-kind leaflet in BMC. Having brought out such an educative material, Mr Panja became highly elated, so much so that he spoke about this leaflet to the borough executive health officers of BMC on two-three occasions, adding this note of appreciation, "Dr Munda has really done a brilliant job for our poor slumdwellers. If our mosquito control workers and other staff of our department read it carefully and spread the information meticulously, people will certainly kill mosquito larvae themselves trying the tricks as suggested by our Munda. Please distribute this leaflet immediately among all concerned . . ."

Dr Nirjan Baker followed his instructions. In the weekly meeting of 15 borough executive health officers held in his chamber on 5 June 2013, he read out the leaflet and asked them to collect it from his office and distribute it among the slumdwellers through their borough mosquito control incharges (BMCI). The borough executive health officers all nodded with a cryptic smile.

About one-and-half-a-month later, while holding meetings with the BMCIs, Munda asked them if they had given the leaflet to their staff for distribution among the slumdwellers. Munda's query made some of the BMCIs disappointed. They said, "We haven't seen the thing yet. Our borough executive health officers are very casual. They do not share with us the proceedings of their meetings at the headquarters of BMC. They are rude and erratic. Some of them are desperately trying to botch up your mosquito abatement programme. If the higher authorities of our corporation do not take stern step against these bad elements, preventing dengue and malaria in the city of Beldanga will be very tough. Please inform this to the MMIC (Health) and request him to look into this matter very seriously. Our CMHO is not an aggressive administrator. Nobody is scared of him. Since he is a medical man, he will never go against another medical man."

Back to his office, Munda rang up Dr Nirjan Baker and shared his observation with him. He listened to Munda and forgot. And Munda knew the reason. It was the planned offense committed by some of his brethren. How could a medical man of BMC enjoy the MMIC's appreciation for the work done by a non-medical person (Munda)?

Sir, forgive them, they're your brethren

Sir Ronald Ross was a British doctor. He was born on 13 May in1857 at Almora (India) near the Himalayan Mountains. On 20 August 1897, he discovered a malaria parasite's stage of development which was the link between humans and mosquitoes and he named this very day of August 'Mosquito Day'. For this epoch making discovery, Sir Ronald Ross was awarded the Nobel Prize in Medicine in 1902. In addition to his Nobel Prize and many other honorary awards, Ross was knighted in 1911. This great scientist died on 16 September in 1932 in London, England.

We all need to remember that in 1899, Sir Ross propounded a theory which states that since malaria is spread by mosquitoes, the disease can be controlled by killing mosquitoes. Initially, critics apart, his contemporaries too were against him. They derided his mosquito theory. They said areas declared free from mosquito breeding would be reinvaded from beyond and that getting rid of every mosquito from an area was a hopeless endeavour.

Ross had to work very hard to substantiate his claim. Prior to getting evidence from the field, Ross turned to mathematics, using the inverse square law, in the form of the 'Drunkard's Walk', to explain that the likely distance and degree of reinvasion from outside wouldn't vitiate attempts at abatement. To dispel the other doubt about mosquito control, Ross constructed an epidemiological model of transmission and successfully showed that it was unnecessary to persist down to the last mosquito. If mosquito densities were reduced below a threshold level, the rate of getting new infections would fall below the rate at which infected people recover, and malaria would gradually die. This 'Threshold Theory' has transcended the limit of time and space.

But the saddest part of the story is that the health officials of our times, more particularly those who are directly looking after malaria control projects in different districts, municipalities, corporations of India, by and large are not aware of the thoughts and propositions of Sir Ronald Ross for prevention of malaria. How many of them have heard about the Mosquito Theory of Ross? So far I have interviewed as many as 50 qualified doctors (having the degrees of MBBS and DPH) working in different parts of the state of West Bengal and asked them whether they had known about this theory? The answer I got from them was terrible! All said, "No . . ." My own perception about those health officials is: None of them is interested in preventing malaria by reducing the population of the offending mosquito. They simply pretend to be public health employees but aren't, in true sense.

Doctors around the country believe only in treating individual patients of malaria, not uprooting the cause of the illness from the society. Which is why, they neglect all sorts of preventive activities needed to prevent the spread of the disease.

Entomologists, on the other hand, want to destroy mosquitoes for preventing transmission of malaria. Presumably, this remains the prime reason why the medical fraternity of our country has traditionally been trying to prevent entomologists from getting recruited in different state health departments of the country.

The controlling health officials around the country are well aware that if entomologists enter the battlefield and get a go-ahead from the policy-makers to steer the fight against mosquito control activities so needed to prevent malaria and other mosquito-borne diseases, the traditional presence of doctors in the battlefield will prove absolutely meaningless and the people will start questioning their credibility about the job of mosquito control that they have long been monitoring without having required knowledge about the subject. Had Sir Ronald been alive, he would have been shocked by seeing the extent of negligence shown by the people of his own fraternity in different states of India towards the preventive aspect of malaria containment. Changing such detrimental scenario is tough unless the political leaders of the country intervene.

As an entomologist, I can only say, "Just forgive them, Sir, they're your brethren."

VOICE FOR MOSQUITOES

In a minority-inhabited ward of Beldanga Municipal Corporation (BMC), cases of malaria had been steeply rising. A team of experts from the ministry of health and family welfare, Government of India, while making house-to-house checks in the area for breeding sources of the city's prime malaria spreading mosquito *Anopheles stephensi*, came across some tanneries wherein overhead water tanks were lying uncovered and the water in them was brimming with the larvae of *Anopheles stephensi*.

The inspection over, the Central team asked the health department of BMC to check those tanneries on a regular basis for mosquito larvae. And the search began accordingly. The concerned mosquito control workers of BMC made weekly visits to the area over a period of 2-3 months. Unfortunately, the situation remained unchanged. Promises made by tannery-owners to take corrective measures were not kept. Overhead water tanks remained open. Mosquito procreation in them was going unchecked. People living in the adjoining areas were facing the consequence. Malaria was spreading fast among them. The ward medical officer (MO) and his mosquito control squads were feeling helpless. Due to their political connections with the local ward councillor and MLA, owners of the tanneries were not bothering at all to listen to the antimosquito guidelines of the corporation.

On 1 August 2013, after knowing this from the concerned BMC-staff, Dr Nirjan Baker, chief municipal health officer (CMHO), discussed the issue with Dr Animesh Munda, entomologist, and asked him to check the tanneries by sending a surveillance team from his office. A verbal order to serve legal notices against the offenders too was given to him by Dr Baker.

After getting the nod from his CMHO, Munda turned overenthusiastic. On the following day, Munda sent one surveillance team to the place. The team made a thorough inspection of all tanneries in the area and informed their findings to Munda from fields on phone. The telephonic conversation between Animesh Munda and the captain of the surveillance team is here.

Standing on the rooftop of a tannery, the captain said to Munda, "Sir, the situation here is horrible! Tanneries have become a big source of *Anopheles stephensi*. Overhead water tanks are open in many tanneries and they are all heavily infested with mosquito larvae. Some tannery-owners are very adamant. They are not listening to us. Solving such a problem is very tough. They are illiterate and unruly. One of them has already threatened us to leave the place immediately. What should we do now? The place is not safe for us. We are feeling quite nervous here."

"Don't be," Munda thundered. "Issue a notice against that idiot. Right now. Unless you punish them, they won't respect you."

"Ok, Sir," the captain said. "I'll do it in a minute, Sir."

Having said this, the captain of the surveillance team took out out a form of notice from his bag in promptness and after filling in the form with requisite information, he asked a worker of the tannery to tell him the name of the proprietor of the tannery.

The tannery-worker turned furious. Instead of telling him the name, he gave him a threat. He said, "Leave this place immediately. Our boss is coming. He is very close to the minister Zakir Ahmed. Don't talk about this bullshit notice in front of him. His bodyguard, Sarafat Ali, is a dangerous man. He won't hesitate to use his razor. Better you go back. We will talk to your commissioner Shakil Ahmed . . . A telephonic caution not to serve the notice has also come to me . . ."

The captain came back to office and intimated the story to Munda. Munda rushed to the chamber of CMHO and briefed him on everything. Dr Baker made no response. His attendant gave him the day's last cup. Dr Baker finished the cup, stood up from his chair and left his office, muttering, "Theirs is the voice in favour of mosquitoes . . . Ours is against, hence it's weaker, much weaker, Animesh . . ."

GORGAS: THE UNSUNG HERO

Mosquito control is not a lowly task. If we accomplish it meticulously, preventing transmission of a mosquito-borne disease is very much possible. The man who first proved this was none but a US Army Physician and the 22nd Surgeon General of the US Army, named William Crawford Gorgas.

Born on 3 October in 1854 in Alabama, William Crawford Gorgas is best known for his outstanding mosquito control activities in Florida, Havana and at the Panama Canal in abating transmission of yellow fever and malaria by implementing efforts on destruction of mosquito breeding sites as the method to conquer them at a time when there was considerable scepticism and opposition to such measures from all around the world. Ultimately in 1904, Gorgas's success in Cuba led him to the fledgling Republic of Panama. This work was so impressive that later it was suggested that entrance to the Panama Canal should be flanked by the statues of Gorgas and Sir Ronald Ross.

William Crawford Gorgas received an honorary knighthood from the King George V at the Queen

Alexandra Military Hospital in the United Kingdom shortly before his death there on 3 July in 1920.

Flashback: Entrusted with the job of constructing a canal through the Isthmus of Panama, a French engineering company came to Panama in 1881 and started working. Till 1889, they tried hard to get the job done but failed abysmally. The failure was primarily due to the devastating onslaught of two mosquito-borne diseases—yellow fever and malaria. Within a span of eight years after the commencement of the construction work, malaria alone caused deaths of as many as 5000 construction workers and cost the company a hefty loss of $US 200 million. Panic-stricken people of the French company fled from Panama, leaving their job unaccomplished. In 1897, the world first came to know from the discovery of Sir Ronald Ross that mosquito is behind malaria.

In 1904, the Americans purchased from the French Canal Company its rights and properties for $US 40 million and resumed the construction work. William Crawford Gorgas joined the project at the behest of his higher bosses. The onus of protecting construction workers from mosquito-borne diseases was assigned to him.

Gorgas arrived in Panama in 1904 along with his troops. After making a prompt assessment of the problem, he planned strategies and began implementing them like a military operation. Gorgas took these measures to improve the situation: 1. Prompt quinine therapy to all febrile patients. 2. Screening of houses to prevent mosquitoes from entering bedrooms. 3. Compelling people to sleep in tents, railroad cars fitted with finely-meshed nets. 4. Draining of swamps and other such mosquito breeding sites or treating them with a locally developed insecticide called Panama Canal Larvicide, which was made of carbolic acid (675 L), powdered resin (90 Kg), caustic soda (13.5 Kg) and water (27 L).

Gorgas worked in Panama till the completion of the project in 1914. The amount he spent for mosquito control was $US 3 million. The results obtained were brilliant! The number of malaria victims among the working force downslided from a staggering 800 per 1000 workers in 1904 to a commendable 40 per 1000 workers in 1914. The casualty figure slumped to 8.7 per 1000 patients from a heart-breaking 40.

By winning the battle against malaria, Gorgas saved America some 40 million mandays of sickness and prevented as many as 71000 deaths in those 10 years of canal-construction. Like that of malaria, the scenario of yellow fever too improved phenomenally, and this came as the collateral benefit of his anti-malaria activities.

People of Panama heaved a sigh of relief. The story of this thumping victory spread across the country and Gorgas became a national hero. Following the recommendation of the then US President Theodore Roosevelt, he was promoted to the rank of general from major. Oxford University conferred an honorary Doctor of Science degree on him. Pertinently, Gorgas got a lot of tacit support from many influential persons around the country, including the US President Theodore Roosevelt, in implementing his plans for mosquito control in Panama.

Clearly, preventing mosquito-borne diseases is feasible if control strategies are planned on the basis of needs and there is a strong political will to support the programme.

Different state health ministers of India and other Southeast Asian countries ought to learn a lesson from this story. Doctors of India, more particularly those who still do not believe Sir Ronald's proposition of malaria control by mosquito abatement can learn a lesson from this story.

OMAN CONQUERS MALARIA

For Oman, it's a dream come true. The government of Oman has wiped out malaria from that country by quelling the offending mosquitoes in a move that lends the lie to the general impression that accomplishing such a task is literally impossible.

Located in the Arabian peninsula, the Sultanate of Oman sprawls over 3,14,000 square kilometres and has a population of 2.5 million distributed over 59 wilayats. Administratively, it is divided into 10 regions—Musandam, North and South Batinah, North and South Sharquiya, Al-Dakhliya, Al-Dahira, Al-Wusta, Dhofar and Masirah Island. Save for the island, the others each have one directorate of health services and one regional reference hospital. Besides, there are 101 health centres, 4 extended health centres and 24 well-equipped hospitals. These health centres cater to the needs of each wilayat.

Employees at the hospitals and peripheral health centres are sincere, honest and disciplined, unlike their brethren in India and elsewhere. They work for the country and are well paid. Those reluctant to toe this rigid line are dismissed and no excuses excepted. Work or quit—the government of Oman knows no other language. There is no funds crunch, nor are there any other constraints.

Around the 1980s, Oman witnessed a virulent resurgence of malaria. Around 0.3 million people suffered every year from malaria. Nearly 98% of them suffered from the dreaded version of the disease called falciparum malaria.

To tackle the situation, Oman's health department intensified all measures needed to reduce the populations of malaria spreading mosquitoes, apart from providing facilities for prompt treatment of the disease. This yielded astounding results and the government stepped up the programme to eradicate the disease in August 1991, laying emphasis on the destruction of *Anopheles culicifacies, Anopheles fluviatilis* and *Anopheles stephensi*, malaria-carriers all. These steps included: 1. Weekly treatment of all mosquito breeding sites with an insecticide called temephos at the rate of 1 ppm (part per million), covering an area of 549 million square metres under the technical guidance and active supervision of trained personnel. 2. Regular disinfection of aircraft and ships to exclude the possibility of infective mosquitoes being brought in from outside. 3. The introduction of larvivorous fish (Guppy and Gambusia) in perennial water bodies. 4. Systematic indoor residual spraying with a highly effective insecticide called lambdacyhalothrin (@ 25 mg/m^2) to protect the population at risk. 5. The use of permethrin-impregnated mosquito nets to provide extra safeguard against infective mosquito-bites.6. Prompt spraying with a herbal product called pyrethrum, following the detection of an indigenous case of malaria to prevent transmission of the disease among the local people.

As a consequence of the country's endeavour, the transmission of malaria has almost stopped. Oman now records around 1,000 cases of malaria a year, a situation that stems more from expatriates, illegal immigrants— imported cases.

Oman has proved that money is mightier than malaria. Since 1991, the country has spent on an average seven US$/head/year to fight the menace; the amount is as much as 16.6% higher than earmarked by the World Health Organization for malaria eradication.

But India's is a frustrating story! The amount spent here hardly exceeds 0.1 US$. More than 70% of the annual budget for malaria control is spent on buying insecticides and the infrastructure is far from adequate. Besides, entomologists who are supposed to plan and execute anti-mosquito measures are not available and where available, they are not allowed to operate independently. Entomologists here work under doctors who know nothing about mosquitoes. An impasse, in the true sense.

Given the comparison, will Oman's success story evoke good response from the bosses here? At least, one hopes so!

Pregnancy attracts mosquitoes

───────

"O shit!" Trisha took a swipe at the winged thing on her neck and put the pulped remains on a sheet of paper. Then, having made a head count, she cried, "Fifteen in ten minutes, God, that's horrible! I'm not staying here any more. Look, the room is full of them . . ."

". . . Still it's much better than yours," Sutapa boasted of her locality.

"What?" Trisha mocked, "Ours is a haven, ma, haven. People sleep there without bednets, do you know that?"

"I know, I know," Sutapa nodded. "You instead use things which guarantee you nothing but a pseudo protection. Have you forgotten so quickly? Why did both your father-and mother-in-laws suffer? Hu? That's not a haven for man, sona, it's haven for malaria, understand? Anyway, when do they come and make a meal of us?" She asked with a cryptic smile.

"Who are you talking about?" asked Trisha, a bit confused.

"In just two years you have forgotten the name of our city queen? Ha!" Sutapa exclaimed.

───────

Trisha thought for some while and then gushed, "Got it! *Anopheles stephensi*, isn't it?"

"Yes," Sutapa shook her head. "Pregnant females of this community normally start their blood sucking business after 10 pm and continue till 4 am. Since they come in very small numbers, the inhabitants of your area and many other places around Beldanga consider themselves luckier than us and hence they always make a bloomer by using those phoney repellents. Had all of those areas been badly infested with menacing mosquitoes such as *Culex* and *Armigeres* like ours, it would have been a different story; malaria would not have been as rampant as is now. But here, we are in absolute peace, people hardly suffer. Which one is better, ours or yours . . . ?"

Before Sutapa could finish, the doorbell rang, Cri-i-i-ng . . .

"Must be your Baba."

Sutapa looked through the peep-hole and opened the door.

A thin, short, dark-complexioned balding man in his late fifties—Dr Dwijen Saha—entered, a bagful of green vegetables in one hand, a packet in the other.

Sutapa took the market-bag from him and entered the kitchen, asking, "Will you take tea?"

"Yes," Dwijen nodded with his eyes, and then, sitting on the sofa beside his daughter, began to wipe his perspiring brow with a handkerchief. "Oh! It's too humid today. Unbearable."

"What is that, Baba?" asked Trisha, staring the covered object beside her father.

"Something very special," Dwijen whispered. "It's very nice."

Trisha unwrapped the packet. "Mosquito net!" She exclaimed with a tinge of unhappiness. "But what for? I won't use this. Impossible. The old habit is dead."

"Don't be silly, Trisha," Dwijen snapped. "You are now at a higher risk of contracting malaria. Mosquitoes target pregnant women. Do you know that?"

"No," Trisha turned curious.

After a brief pause, Dwijen explained, "Scientists from Durham and Aberdeen Universities have indeed done a brilliant job. Have you heard the name Gambia?"

"Yes," Trisha nodded. "A highly malarious African country."

"Yes!" Dwijen's gratification was apparent. "You are absolutely right. Led by Dr Steve Lindsay, malaria expert, the researchers did the work. They built identical huts and employed the help of pregnant and non-pregnant women, asking them to sleep in the huts under mosquito nets. In the morning, they collected mosquitoes from the huts for a couple of days and then, by analysing the data, estimated how attractive the tiny tormentors found each woman. The results were most startling. On an average, twice as many mosquitoes crowded the huts of the pregnant women compared to women who were not expecting."

"Is that so?" Trisha shuddered. "But why? I mean, why were the bloody monsters so fond of the pregnant women?"

"For three reasons," said Dwijen gravely. "First, it is said that in the later stages of pregnancy, women need more oxygen and hence they breathe more heavily—approximately 20% more. And this increase of rate of respiration results in a greater production of carbon dioxide and other such attractants that help the tiny terrorists easily find their prey. The second reason is . . ." Dwijen paused and glanced back.

Sutapa gave him a cup of tea. Having sipped from it, he continued, "Yes, another reason . . . a woman's body temperature rises slightly during pregnancy, with blood flow to the skin boosted to help her cool down. This may increase the release of substances from the skin, perhaps in perspiration, making her more attractive to the insects.

"The third point is the women's behaviour. The pregnant women were found to leave the relative safety of their mosquito net-covered bed, on an average, twice as much during the night, probably to go to the toilet.

"Mosquitoes are really very discerning creatures. They can spend hours together sitting on the outer wall of a mosquito net for a single drop of your blood. Their noses are very powerful. They can smell their prey from even a distance of 35 metres, remember this."

"Nose!" Trisha burst out laughing, "Mosquitoes have noses, hah, hah . . . ! What does it look like, Baba?"

"Very delicate. Some scientists abroad had the chance of noticing it in the case of the dengue-bearing mosquito *Aedes aegypti* under a scanning electron microscope."

"Who?"

"Martin Geier and Hinrich Sab at the University of Regensburg, both biologists of international repute. By the by, have you ever really noticed a mosquito's antennae?"

"No."

"Wait," Dwijen smiled. "I will show you."

Having said this, he switched off the fan, swatted the life out of a mosquito and, putting the remains on a glossy white paper on the table, took out a magnifying glass from a drawer and asked her to take note.

Curious, Trisha watched.

". . . See the head?" Dwijen asked rather impatiently.

"Yes, yes," Trisha shook her head after a brief silence.

"Good. Now look at the two hair like structures in front of the head, each coming out from the side of an eye . . . see it?"

"Y-yes got it! They're very fine."

"That's the thing I was talking about," Dwijen took a long breath, paused and then smilingly said, "Every mosquito has two such appendages called antennae or feelers. In case of *Aedes aegypti*, they are about two millimetres long and each of them is completely covered with some 1,000 tiny sensory hairs."

"Hairs on a hair!" Trisha was wide-eyed.

"Yes," he continued. "And these hairs, each containing several sensory cells with different receptors for odours, have varying structures—five different kinds were detected—and functions. The majority . . . just a sec . . ." Dwijen stopped here for some time, put a zarda paan into his mouth, and then, after having chewed it for a while, resumed, "Hu, the majority by far some 800, are receptive to odour signals. These are called chemoreceptors and they assume the responsibility of the nose in a mosquito. Other sensory hairs on the antennae react to warmth (thermoreceptors), and still others to motoric inpulses (mechanoreceptors).

"When a sensory cell, I mean, a chemoreceptor, 'perceives' an odour, it transmits the information in the form of an electrical impulse via the nerve to the central nervous system, from where comes the final instructions, either 'Go back, go back' or 'Attack, attack' . . . Is everything clear to you? Right. So, be cautious and learn. Or else, your baby will suffer. Do you know how many babies die in their mothers' wombs every year in Africa because of malaria induced low-birth-weight associated problems?

"A heart-stopping figure! It stands somewhere between 1,00,000 and 2,00,000. Millions and millions of people around the world cannot afford to buy a mosquito net, but here, privileged people like you sniff at it. It's bad. Very bad."

"Forgive me Baba, I'll use it from now on," Trisha said, her promise not quite hiding the smug complacency in her voice, "but shall I ask you one question?"

"Sure," Dwijen nodded.

"Will it really be needed for us, Baba? Sanjay and me live on the fifth floor of our building. Isn't the chance of getting bitten by mosquitoes zero there?"

"Oh no, you're absolutely wrong," the response was electric. "Her character is just the reverse. *Anopheles stephensi* is geophobic. Given the chance, this villainous piece always prefers higher storeys for spawning, unlike *Aedes aegypti* and *Culex quinquefasciatus* which are geophilic. *Anopheles stephensi* can breed at the height of 100 feet of a building, too. What does that tell you?"

There was no reply.

"What . . . Trisha . . . ?" Dwijen persisted.

"Uh," Trisha's reverie broke. "It means dwellers of the city's sky-scrapers too have no way of escaping her attack. How devious! I must tell Rahul. He's arriving the day after tomorrow."

"O, yes," Dwijen insisted, "tell him to bring some permethrin-soap. In America, this is widely available."

"Permethrin . . . !" Trisha wondered.

"Yes," he explained, "it's very useful soap for pregnant women. If you use this after taking a bath, the smell of permethrin will linger on your skin for several hours and make you repulsive, so much so that the tiny terrorists will turn up their noses and fly away for fear of death . . ."

Suddenly there was a call from Sutapa. "Your bread is ready . . ."

"Yes, coming . . ." Dr Dwijen Saha, a veteran science reporter of the Times of India, stood up and walked into the toilet, muttering, "Sleeping with mosquito net should be made mandatory especially for the pregnant women living in each and every high-risk malarious area around the world."

Human transport of dengue

From one man to another, a dengue virus is transmitted through the bites of *Aedes* mosquitoes and we all are aware of this. But sometimes the reverse also occurs and most of us do not know this. Yes, a man himself can transport the dengue virus from an *Aedes* mosquito to another mosquito. Got stunned? You may be. But it's true.

As you know, if a dengue virus-carrying *Aedes* mosquito bites a man today, the virus will enter his body following the mosquito-bite and 4 to 11 days later, the man will develop fever, the first symptom of dengue. And after catching fever, the patient will stop doing his normal work, opt for blood-test and seek medical help for recovery. Unless one catches fever, nobody thinks of testing blood for malaria or dengue. According to experts, the virus of dengue starts circulating in the blood of a man at least 2 days before the onset of fever and during these two days, the man does not feel any physical discomfort and hence bothers not to go for any medical check-up. These 2 days are very dangerous because during this period of time, a person carrying a dengue virus in his blood feels normal and hence the person remains undiagnosed. And it's during these 2 days a person such as this travels to another place in an aircraft and after reaching there, acts as a source of dengue virus; the local mosquitoes bite him, pick up the dengue virus from his blood and spread it among the locals.

Transmission of dengue among the local people due to air arrivals has already been pointed out in some countries of the Americas. For instance, in 2000, local people in Cuba, Dominican Republic, Jamaica and Puerto Rico had suffered from dengue @ 1.2, 40.7, 0.9 and 62.8 per 100,000 population consequent upon 1.741, 2.972, 1.323 and 3.341 million international air arrivals to these countries respectively. You will be surprised to know that in Singapore, population growth (from 2.1 million in 1970 to 5 million in 2009) apart, rapid increase in the number of air passengers has been identified as a major challenge in fighting against dengue. The number of air travellers to Singapore was only 1.7 million in 1970. The figure rose to a staggering 18 million in 2009 and it's now far more than that.

Going by a report, published in the March 2013 issue of an internationally reputed medical journal Public Health, a stunning 2500 million people now travel in aircraft globally in each year. How many of them carry dengue virus in their blood? We don't know. In fact, answering such question is very tough. Is any device for detecting a dengue virus within a fraction of a second available? No. And hence preventing human transport of dengue virus from one place to another within the same country or from one country to another is literally not possible.

One needs to remember that the number of dengue cases is fast increasing around the world. Poverty, population growth, lack of political commitment, irresponsible disposal of modern products (plastic, tyres), climate changes, lack of planning and trained human resources, increased global travel are associated with dengue. The disease is spreading to previously uninfected areas. The cost for treatment of one patient of dengue now varies from US$ 600 to US$ 1,500.

Situation is grim. When will our political leaders understand this?

DENGUE DOES NOT ANNOY THEM

Thousands of them were wriggling in a well on the premises of an old three-storey building in north Kolkata. A field worker from the health department of Kolkata Municipal Corporation (KMC) took out a sample of water from the well and showed it to the KMC's consultant entomologist, Dr Vivek Roy (original name changed).

Having noticed the things, Dr Roy admonished, "What the hell are you doing here! Why didn't you serve him a legal notice?"

After a brief silence, the field worker said shakily, "It's not possible, Sir. The councillor of this ward has warned us not to disturb his voters by issuing any notice. He is a very dangerous man. My service will be at stake if we go against him, Sir.'

"Is the landlord at home now?"

"Maybe, Sir."

"Call him, quick."

Minutes later, a short obese man in his early fifties, Mr Deshmukh Pandey, appeared, chewing paan (betel-leaf). "Yes, what can I do for you, doctor?" he asked.

"No, Mr Pandey, you needn't do anything for me," Dr Roy said. "You instead take care of this well. Do you know which mosquito is breeding here? *Aedes aegypti*. And this mosquito spreads dengue, chikungunya . . . So, please do seal it immediately."

"Impossible!" Mr Pandey derided. Then, pointing to the small rooms around the courtyard, he pleaded, "People living here are all my tenants. They use water from this well for their domestic purposes. How can I seal it? Will your corporation fulfil their needs?"

"Then release some fish," Dr Roy offered gloomily.

"Fish?" Mr Pandey exclaimed. "No, no, it's not possible. There are many widows in this house. They will not allow me to do this . . ."

"Ok, ok," Dr Roy cut him short. "Can you buy some expanded polystyrene (EPS) beads?"

"Why not?" Mr Pandey volunteered.

"Fine, then do it immediately. The EPS beads are very useful. Just put the beads in it (@ 500-1000 gm/m^2 surface area and see how nicely they cover the surface of the water and prevent mosquito breeding. The EPS beads will float on water surface in several layers. Since mosquitoes lay eggs on the surface of water, the physical barrier formed by the blanket of EPS beads will prevent them from doing so. The immatures of mosquitoes (larvae and pupae) trapped under the blanket of EPS beads will die of suffocation. And there will no mosquito procreation in this well."

"Brilliant!" Mr Pandey gushed. "Give me just 24 hours time, I'll do it."

"Okay, go ahead . . ."

Having said this, Dr Roy left the building. At the entry to the premises, suddenly he heard an elderly voice calling him from behind. He stopped and glanced back.

The old man came nearer and whispered, "This is the fifth time he has made such commitment. But, rest assured, he will never do it."

"Hmm," Dr Roy shook his head and then, pompously saying "let's see", entered the next building. There, too, after detecting the larvae of *Aedes* larvae in a bitumen drum, he called the landlord and asked gravely, "What is this?"

"Aqua-worms . . ."

"What!"

"Yes. We see them in our water throughout the year. They come along with the corporation water. What can I do? It's your fault."

"Listen," Dr Roy snapped. "These are not aqua-worms. These are mosquito larvae, the larvae of the dengue spreading mosquito *Aedes aegypti*. And remember, they don't come along with the water of KMC. You people help them grow. They are born in your containers where you store water for days together, understand? So please overturn it immediately."

So saying, he walked into the next house, where his men had been waiting for him standing by the side of a masonry tank; it was full of mosquito larvae, mostly of the breed *Aedes aegypti*. Dr Roy saw the tank and asked the house-owner, "Why don't you remove water from this tank at a weekly interval?"

The house-owner—a thin balding man of around seventy years old—turned furious. "Mr, rectify your own loopholes first and then drill us. Do you know how much water do we actually need and how much does your corporation supply? Ask your mayor to fulfil our needs first and then talk about the removal of water from tanks."

Dr Roy waited there for some while, staring the face of the old-timer and then, asking his staff to check other houses, left for office.

The story told here is not fictitious. It's exactly what has been going in many places around the city for long. Despite being requested by the mosquito control staff of KMC, many people here hardly bother to remove mosquitogenic conditions in their houses. And this remains one of the main reasons why dengue suddenly breaks out here and there across the city.

Tracking down the pages of history, classical dengue (DF) first broke out in Kolkata in 1824 and then reappeared in 1836, 1903, 1904, 1905 and 1911. The episode of DF in an epidemic form first occurred here in July 1923, which persisted till September of that year. About 40% of the city's population suffered the brunt in those three months. After that, the city did not face any major outbreak of DF for a period of long six decades. But, suddenly, in July 1983, dengue again broke out here almost like a comet, affecting thousands of people.

The incidence of dengue haemorrhagic fever (DHF) first occurred here in July 1963. Transmission of the disease continued till March 1964. About 0.1 million people became infected. Most of them were children. Five hundred patients were hospitalised. Two hundred of them died. Then, after remaining quiescent over the period of a long two and half a decade, DHF again unveiled its ugly face in this city in October 1990. Officially 60 children became infected, of whom 12 succumbed.

In the past 8 years (2005-2012), altogether 7569 people of Kolkata became infected with dengue and 21 of them died. The year-wise break-up is: 3546 cases of dengue with 12 deaths in 2005, 394 cases with 1 death in 2006, 30 cases with zero death in 2007, 184 cases with 3 deaths in 2008, 263 cases with zero death in 2009, 960 cases with 3 deaths in 2010, 340 cases with zero death in 2011 and 1852 cases with 2 deaths in 2012.

Unfortunately, dengue does not bother the people of Kolkata. Had they been concerned, they would have been proactive. Is preventing dengue by KMC alone feasible given the people's lackadaisical attitude?

PREVENTING DENGUE

Dengue is a mosquito-borne acute flu-like viral infection caused by a virus of the genus Flavivirus. So far four strains of the dengue virus have been identified around the world and these are termed as Den1, Den 2, Den 3 and Den 4. Based on symptoms, dengue is of two types, classical dengue fever (DF) and dengue haemorrhagic fever (DHF). Of the two, DF is non-fatal and it develops following the infection caused by any strain of the dengue virus. On the contrary, DHF is fatal and it develops when a person sequentially gets infected with two strains of the dengue virus within a span of six months.

Primarily spread by the mosquito *Aedes aegypti*, dengue has reemerged as a grave international public health problem. Reasons that seem to have facilitated such virulent resurgence, are: 1. Widespread increase in the number of automobiles creating numerous new types of breeding sites for *Aedes aegypti*. 2. Unbridled urbanisation. 3. Population growth. 4. Deterioration of public health infrastructure. 5. Lack of effective mosquito control. 6. Increased air travel. 7. Shipping and trade. 8. Insecticidal resistance. 9. Lack of political will.

There is no specific treatment for dengue, nor has any effective vaccine been developed yet against the disease. Given the situation, reduction of *Aedes aegypti* population is a must for prevention and control of the disease. And we could easily achieve this by employing some common-sense approaches. For example, unused containers kept outside may be placed indoors or under a shed so that rainwater does not accumulate in them. Household and garden utensils (buckets, bowls and watering devices) kept outdoors may be turned upside down when not in use to prevent accumulation of rainwater. Ant-traps used to protect food storage cabinets can be filled with salty water instead of fresh water. Ornamental pools, fountains and basement water tanks could be stuffed with guppy, tilapia or any other such larvivorous fish. Demolition of abandoned water tanks and sealing of unused wells too are easily practicable for us.

Sometimes a small flower vase becomes a source of danger in case water in the vase remains unchanged. To make it safe, what should we do? Nothing big of any sort. We just need to change its water at weekly intervals.

Masonry tank in Kolkata and many other cities around the country is a common source of *Aedes aegypti*. Unless the tank is emptied and scrubbed at weekly intervals, tackling the problem is tough. Scrubbing of the tank is needed because if one does not do this, the eggs of *Aedes aegypti*, that can withstand desiccation for a period of more than one year, will remain glued to its inner surfaces and begin to hatch as soon as the tank is refilled with water. Likewise, small water storage containers such as plastic or iron drums, buckets, vats, pitchers, barrels, empty battery shells and tin cans too welcome dengue spreading mosquitoes to procreate therein if we keep them open. We could avert this problem simply by covering them with tight lids or screen.

Following heavy downpour, rainwater in many houses accumulates on their courtyards and rooftops. Simply by stirring the accumulated rainwater with a broom, we could easily prevent mosquito breeding in these places.

In some poorly-built houses, underground water reservoirs are commonly found located below stairs and most of them remain uncovered. Huge breeding of *Aedes aegypti* occurs in these reservoirs throughout the year. To prevent mosquito breeding in such a water reservoir, we need not spray any insecticide. We just need one lid to cover it, nothing else, nothing more.

Heaps of old tyres are very often found lying stacked in the open space at garages (both public and private), tyre retreading centres and other places in different cities/towns around the country. These are fertile breeding grounds of *Aedes aegypti*. Mosquito breeding in such tyres begins when rainwater accumulates in them and the breeding continues till the tyres dry up. Fifty to 500 mosquitoes may emerge from one such tyre in a day. Simply by keeping the tyres under a shed, one could solve this problem. Industrial scraps, broken utensils, coconut shells, earthen teapots, jars, bottles, plastics, domestic wastes and other such discarded materials also create huge problem during the rainy season if they are stacked or thrown in the open space. Consequent upon the accumulation of rainwater in these unwanted items, they all turn into suitable breeding sites for *Aedes aegypti* and many other species of mosquitoes. Hence these materials ought to be destroyed or kept away from populated areas.

At construction sites, mosquito breeding in plastic drums could be checked by keeping them properly covered. Water tanks used for soaking bricks and other construction purposes may be emptied at weekly intervals using pumps. Empty bitumen drums, which we often find lying indisposed after completion of road-repairing work, need to be kept upside down.

Truly, these are all very simple measures and we need to take them throughout the year to prevent procreation of the dengue spreading mosquitoes in and around our houses. But during an outbreak of dengue, some short-term anti-mosquito measures too have to be taken to exclude the possibilities of being infected with the disease. These two, in particular, seem to be of much help. 1. Spraying of bedrooms with commercially available safe aerosols. 2. Liberal use of mosquito repellents such as mats, coils, creams and liquid vaporisers.

General people apart, the local health authorities too have to take some measures to prevent dengue, especially these five ones: pinpointing disease transmission areas based on the data obtained from various sources such as government hospitals, nursing homes and private pathological laboratories, making house-to-house inspection in every dengue-prone area at weekly intervals for detection and elimination of mosquito breeding sites, killing of *Aedes aegypti* larvae by spraying temephos 50% EC (organophosphorous compound) in all those domestic water containers that cannot be managed by the general people; filing of cases against individual private house-owners, building contractors and developers, hospital authorities, garage-owners, owners of tyre retreading centres and other such people in violation of antimosquito guidelines issued by the civic authorities; and conducting mass awareness campaign through electronic and other effective media.

We all need to remember that mosquitoes could breed in as little as ½ cm of water. Studies by entomologists have revealed that if we could somehow manage to keep the Breteau index of *Aedes aegypti* (i.e. the number of water containers with *Aedes aegypti* larvae per 100 houses) at or below 5 in our environment, we will have lower risk of contracting dengue. Can't we achieve this? Of course we can. And for that we need to ensure that there would be no mosquitogenic source in and around our houses any more.

And now, to conclude, let me frankly append: mosquito control in countries like India is still considered a lowly task. Those who plan and implement strategies against mosquitoes do virtually know very little about the subject. And sadly, the government initiatives to deploy entomologists so needed to steer mosquito control activities are not yet in sight. Improving such dispiriting situation is very tough unless political leaders intervene.

POWER OF POLITICS

66 **A**s per the government policy, if any
o o o confirmed case of dengue is reported
from a household, fogging with a herbal insecticide
called pyrethrum (2% extract) ought to be carried out
in 50 households surrounding the one from where the
incidence of dengue has been reported. In the midst
of July in 2012, following the sudden outbreak of this
mosquito-borne disease in some wards of BMC (Beldanga
Municipal Corporation), Jagannath Panja, member of
the mayor-in-council (Health) of BMC, by issuing a
communiqué, asked all the concerned health officials of
his department to take this antimosquito measure within
24 hours following the occurrence of a case of dengue
anywhere in the city of Beldanga. Mosquito control
squads working in different wards of BMC began working
accordingly.

"Initially, the fogging operation was running quite
smoothly. But the story took a quick twist in a ward in the
central part of the city. Councillor of the ward, Moinul
Ahmed, suddenly asked the medical officer of his ward to
take fogging measure everywhere in his ward, irrespective
of the occurrence of any case of dengue. The officer was
asked to take such measure twice a week. Since Mr
Ahmed was the borough chairman, he asked the other

ward medical officers to do the same in their wards under the borough of Mr Ahmed. Quite obviously, mosquito control workers and the ward MOs of the borough became disappointed. But they could not ignore the instructions of Mr Ahmed. In fact, no one in the health department of BMC had the courage to ignore his instructions. Even the chief municipal health officer of BMC too was scared of Mr Ahmed. Since he was foul-mouthed, health officials of BMC would not contradict him.

"The fogging operation continued over a period of long 2 months in the ward of Mr Ahmed and other wards of his borough, causing a huge wastage of public money. But nobody bothered. Nobody stood against the detrimental whip of Mr Ahmed. Even Jagannath Panja himself did not try to stop Mr Ahmed from committing such a serious offence in the name of fighting against dengue. How many confirmed cases of dengue were reported last year from the ward of Mr Ahmed? Mr Ahmed had no answer.

"As the news of indiscriminate fogging in different wards of the borough of Mr Ahmed spread to different areas of Beldanga, some other ward councillors too started running the show just to satisfy their innocent voters. Until December 2012, many ward councillors having no inkling of the subject behaved like adepts in the subject of mosquito control. One day I met one such ward councillor and frankly asked him as to why he was so keen on running fogging operation in his ward unnecessarily. With a cryptic smile, the councillor said, 'Mr Munda, we know that fogging is a puerile exercise. You will advise us not to allow this. But we will never listen to you. We will keep doing this because, only by carrying out this hollow activity, we political leaders can easily prove that we work for our voters. General people do not want to know what is good and what is bad. They want us only to deliver for them. The quality of work has no value to them. Our voters want quantity. The more you show, the more is your gain. Mr Munda, I am a chemical engineer and, like you, I do also believe in doing scientific work . . . but that's not possible given the existing socioeconomic conditions of our people.'

"Misuse of political power is a traditional malady in the city of Beldanga. Even an IAS officer here does not have the courage to contradict a political leader . . ." Sitting in his office, Dr Animesh Munda, entomologist, was telling this to a friend who had come to invite him to the wedding ceremony of his daughter. It was in the late afternoon on 5 July 2013. Suddenly, there was a phone-call from a ward councillor, Ms Sumana Das.

Munda received the call in promptness. "Yes, Madam. What can I do for you?"

In a husky voice, the councillor said, "Dengue is spreading very fast in my ward. My voters are scared. Please send your surveillance team tomorrow. Your team is very efficient. Rajib Raha, a resident of 420 Kapalik Road, just opposite my residence, has fallen into the clutches of dengue. His blood report has reached me."

"Ok, I will do. Don't worry."

The day after, Munda's mosquito surveillance team rushed to the place, cancelling its prescheduled visit to a vulnerable area in southern part of the city. The team made a thorough inspection of all sorts of water storage containers in and around 150-160 houses surrounding Rajib Raha's house. But *Aedes* larvae were found only in 2-3 houses. The team also collected a photocopy of Rajib's blood report. His blood was positive for dengue Ig G antibody.

"Shit!" Munda frowned with disgust, looking at the report. "It's not a case of current infection. Very old case. Maybe quite a few years back he became infected with the disease. Our work in the area has all gone to waste!"

Having muttered this to himself, Munda called up the concerned medical officer and asked him whether he had received any phone call from his councillor.

"Yes," the MO replied. "She phoned me yesterday."

"But his was not a case of current infection."

"I know, I know. Still we had to do fogging there. Besides, I met Rajib personally. Field workers of my ward went in a group of 3-4. Borough surveillance team comprising 6 field workers too visited the area. Our staff worked there for more than 2 hours, making house-to-house checks for mosquito larvae. But they found no larvae of dengue mosquito."

"Ok. Thanks."

Munda cut the line and went to the toilet, muttering, "Idiots! They are all out to fuck the country's resources. People ought to shoot them instead of voting them . . ."

MAN SMART, MOSQUITO SMARTER

Due to various reasons—including global warming, change of climate, infrastructural inadequacies, lack of effective mosquito control, insecticidal resistance, unbridled unbanisation, multiplication of the number of automobiles, deforestation, population growth, increased air travel, shipping and trade, lack of people's awareness and war—mosquito-borne ailments are causing havoc around the world.

A staggering 350-500 million people now become infected with malaria every year, of them 1 million die. Most of the global deaths due to malaria occur in Africa. One hundred countries are endemic for this disease. Among the Southeast Asian countries, the worst affected is India, where over 11 lakh cases of malaria with 710 deaths occurred every year during 2009 to 2013 (till July). The country as a whole is endemic for malaria. People of 12 states such as Andhra Pradesh, Assam, Chattisgarh, Gujarat, Jharkhand, Madhya Pradesh, Maharashtra, Meghalaya, Mizoram, Orissa, Rajasthan and West Bengal suffer the brunt more than in the other states of the country.

Another disease of greater concern is dengue. Scenario in India is quite annoying. Officially 1 lakh 53 thousand 96 cases of dengue with 840 deaths were reported from this country during 2007-2013 (till August). As many as 16 states—including Andhra Pradesh, Karnataka, Kerala, Maharashtra, Orissa, Tamil Nadu, Uttar Pradesh and West Bengal—usually report cases of dengue in greater numbers than the other states of the country. Once considered an urban disease, dengue now affects the rural people too.

Another mosquito-borne disease is chikungunya. In India, people of Gujarat, Karnataka, Kerala, Maharashtra, Orissa, Tamil Nadu, West Bengal and Lakshadweep generally suffer more from this ailment than the others. During 2007 to 2013 (till August), 3 lakh 22 thousand 15 people became infected with this disease around the country. Since it is not a fatal disease, people hardly bother about chikungunya.

The deadliest of all insect-borne diseases is Japanese encephalitis (JE). In India, 4163 cases of JE with 732 deaths were officially reported during 2008 to 2013 (till August). As many as 17 states of the country have become saddled with the problem of JE. In four states—Andhra Pradesh, Assam, Uttar Pradesh and Bihar—the situation is quite grim. Most annoying, JE has unveiled its ugly face in Siberia too, the Northeast part of the USSR that remains covered with ice for more than half the year. The mortality rate of JE is high; it ranges from 20 to 50%.

The scenario of lymphatic filariasis too is no less annoying. In India, indigenous cases of filariasis have been reported from 250 districts in 20 states/Union Territories. About 31 million people are harbouring microfilarae (offspring of the causative worm *Wuchereria bancrofti*) in their blood. Twenty-three million people have developed symptoms of the disease. This is a crippling disease. And its principal transmitter is *Culex quinquefasciatus*, a dirty water-breeder whose procreation in third world countries, including India, has long been going unchecked.

Treatment and case management apart, mosquito control is also equally essential for prevention and control of these diseases. But how is this job possible? This remains a billion-dollar question.

In India, many people, including doctors, still have a notion that mosquito control is a very simple job. Anyone can do this. No technical expertise is required for this job. In fact, this overconfidence is the prime reason why transmission of mosquito-borne diseases such as malaria, dengue, chikungunya, Japanese encephalitis and lymphatic filariasis is still going unchecked around the country.

Mosquitoes emerged on this earth over 200 million years ago and they have successfully countered almost every attempt of our invasion, proving themselves enormously adaptable to new threats and environments, and are well-conversant with the Darwin's most fundamental principle of Struggle for Existence.

The first chemical insecticide we used against mosquitoes is DDT. After the World War II, DDT was used by different countries around the world, including India, to prevent transmission of malaria. Initially, the results were brilliant. The incidence of malaria in India downslided phenomenally: from a staggering 75 million cases with 0.8 million deaths in 1951 to a comfortable 50,000 with no death in 1961. Sri Lanka, with 3 million cases of malaria in 1947, had only 29 in 1964. Other countries too got benefited by using DDT. People around the world heaved a sigh of relief.

Following this "miraculous" victory, there were people who believed malaria had been wiped out, but the euphoria didn't last long. With some species of malaria spreading mosquitoes having grown resistant to DDT in some parts of the world in the early 1960s, they were back with a vengeance. And since the 1970s, they've not let up. To tackle the situation, scientists around the world chose other chemical insecticides as alternatives to DDT. But those weapons too lost their efficacy at some point of time.

Besides growing resistant to DDT and other insecticides, mosquitoes have changed their resting habits too, to by-pass the danger. For an instance, the main malaria spreading mosquito of Kolkata, *Anopheles stephensi*, once used to rest indoors before and after imbibing human blood, but now the mosquito does so outdoors.

Anopheles stephensi females enter bedrooms only when they need blood so necessary for them to nourish their eggs. This phenomenal change in the resting habit of the mosquito is presumably due to the excitorepellatory impact of DDT used in this city during the 1950s and 1960s for preventing malaria. Given the situation, destroying *Anopheles stephensi* mosquito by spraying an insecticide indoors is not feasible in the city of Kolkata.

Fogging, as done in many towns and cities around the country as mosquito control measure, is also not effective. Remember, the fog drives mosquitoes away; it does not kill them. People around the country take this measure without getting precise information about the resting and biting habits of mosquitoes.

Some overenthusiastic researchers once even dreamed of combating mosquito menace by sterilising the male mosquitoes through various techniques in the laboratory and then releasing them in fields where they would compete with the normal males for copulating with fertile females. The females inseminated by sterile males would not be able to lay viable eggs.

One must remember that a female mosquito, like other insects, normally mates with her partner only once in her life and following a single sexual intercourse, she remains pregnant till death. It was this characteristic scientists wished to cash in on by developing such a technique. Initially, the trick sounded excellent, but in a study jointly conducted by the World Health Organization and the Indian Council of Medical Research in Delhi in the mid-1970s, it proved absolutely ridiculous and was hence rejected.

For reducing man-mosquito contact, the latest idea is to use insecticide-treated mosquito nets, more precisely the nets treated with a synthetic pyrethroid such as deltamethrin, permethrin, cyfluthrin or lambdacyhalothrin. But in cities like Kolkata, where most people do not even use ordinary mosquito nets for lack of space or sheer reluctance, will this new prescription ever make any sense? Or will such insecticide-treated mosquito nets be effective in areas where malaria-bearing mosquitoes bite exclusively outdoors? No. They won't be.

Killing adult mosquitoes is very tough. Their larvae that live in still water have to be targeted. But accomplishing this too is not easy. Like adults, mosquito larvae too are tricky. Ironically, they're smarter than our kids, for they need no parental care to grow up and they can also battle any adversity for survival on their own. Once considered brahmastra—temephos and fenthion— both are organophosphorous insecicides, have now lost their credibility against mosquito larvae in many countries around the world, including India.

People's enthusiasm about the killing of mosquito larvae by MLO (mosquito larvicidal oil), a 100% petroleum product, is also fast evaporating because of its lesser efficacy in clogged surface drains, roadside-gullies, hyacinth-infested ponds, ditches and other such places that support a greater procreation of the menacing mosquitoes.

In the 1970s, another effective measure was devised by experts using a completely different group of chemical compounds called insect growth regulators (IGRs) that prevents emergence of adult mosquitoes, hindering the normal process of larval growth. For years together, extensive field trials with IGRs were conducted in different countries to evaluate their effectiveness. Initially, they seemed effective, but subsequently, some of the IGRs lost their credibility because of the development of larval resistance. As a result, the approach collapsed, frustrating the scientists who had propounded it.

The role of larvivorous fish, Guppy and Gambusia, too is now increasingly becoming fishy, especially in the cities of developing countries, including India, for genuine reasons of excessive water pollution and clogging of surface drains, ditches, canals and other such breeding sites.

Killing of mosquito larvae by using microbial toxins also does not seem very much promising. Experts have already proved that the larvae of the filariasis spreading mosquito *Culex quinquefasciatus* can grow 150-fold resistant to the toxin of a microbe called *Bacillus sphaericus* following 20-25 rounds of its application within a year, pointing to the fact that this toxin cannot be the weapon of choice for a long-term containment programme of *Culex quinquefasciatus* larvae. Besides, this toxin has a very low efficacy against the larvae of dengue, chikungunya and yellow fever spreading mosquito *Aedes aegypti.*

The toxin of another microbe called *Bacillus thuringiensis israelensis* too has some limitations; it works less in highly polluted water due to its rapid biodegradation caused by water pollution as well as its adsorption on organic particles.

Clearly, neither a chemical insecticide nor a biocontrol agent (fish and microbial toxin) alone can help us reduce mosquito menace. We need an integrated mosquito management, involving judicious use of effective, less polluting insecticides; biocontrol measures; environmental management practices; information, education and communication activities; and enforcement of legal steps to involve people in removing mosquitogenic conditions from their houses and neighbourhood. A superb proposition! But is accomplishing such task possible, especially in countries like India, where doctors having no or very little knowledge about mosquitoes still oversee mosquito control operations, and where the political will is abysmally lacking?

How we help
mosquitoes breed

Water is indispensable to life. Life minus water means death. Surprisingly, many of us do not know that such precious water could also become a source of great danger if we store the water or allow it to remain stored in an open container or place just for seven days. Why? The reason is very simple. The water so stored welcomes mosquitoes to breed therein.

The process of mosquito procreation in stored water occurs in this way: from their hideouts, which are located nowhere else but inside your bedrooms, kitchens, toilet and storerooms, the gravid female mosquitoes silently come closer to the stored water, usually in the evening hours, sit on the water surface and lay their eggs. The eggs are laid singly or in rafts containing 150-200 eggs each. Then, in a day or two, the eggs hatch into larvae, which we commonly call wrigglers. The larvae develop into pupae. Finally, adult mosquitoes fly out from the pupae. The entire process of emergence of adult mosquitoes from eggs takes only a week's time for completion. Unfortunately, many learned people do not know this, nor do they want to know about this from others. Believe it or not, despite being repeatedly requested by the health department of Kolkata Municipal

Corporation (KMC), people of this metropolis have not yet given up the habit of storing water. And this is one of the main reasons why breeding of some dangerous species of mosquitoes in the city's environment goes unabated almost throughout the year. If our beloved fellow-citizens of Kolkata do not change their attitude, improving the city's mosquitogenic situation is very tough. If we want to wage a real war against mosquitoes, we all need to keep a track of some basic information about these tiny winged terrorists.

Remember, mosquitoes do not breed in running water. They always breed in stagnant water. You will be surprised to know that a mosquito is such a creature that it does not require huge volume of water to breed. It can breed in as little as half a centimetre of still water. Unfortunately, people of Kolkata by and large are not aware of this and hence are least bothered. While visiting your neighbouring houses or the houses of your friends or relatives, you must have seen in many of them how water-filled masonry tanks and many other water containers such as drums, earthen vats, earthen barrels, buckets, earthen pitchers and so on are lying uncovered days after days and the people of those houses are silently ignoring them. If people do not change their mindset, preventing mosquito breeding is very tough. Can the mosquito control staff of KMC solve this problem alone? No.

Let me now share with you some of my own experiences that I have gathered from my personal visits to different places across the city as the entomologist of KMC over the past two and half decades. You will be surprised to know that even in some posh areas of the city, I have seen the overhead water tanks in many houses lying open for days together and the house-owners are not putting covers on them in spite of being repeatedly requested by the mosquito control staff of KMC.

In some houses around the city of Kolkata, I have seen overhead water tanks having holes developed on their walls lying unnoticed. Water tanks on the rooftops of some hospitals, colleges, high-rises, residential complexes, office buildings have also been found many a time remaining uncovered or broken with huge number of mosquito larvae wriggling in stored water inside them.

Unused wells brimming with huge number of mosquito larvae too did not escape my eyes during my visits to some places around the city.

Some people keep flower vases in their bedrooms or balconies but they often forget to change water in the vases. As a result, the flower vases turn into breeding places of mosquitoes, more particularly the mosquitoes that spread dengue and chikungunya.

During rainy season and the times thereafter, accumulated rainwater on rooftops of many houses, office buildings, hospitals, educational institutions, hostels, low-lying lands, courtyards and other such places turns into another big source of danger.

Tyres, coconut shells, tin cans, broken bottles and other such discarded items too turn into suitable breeding sites for mosquitoes following the accumulation of rainwater in them. But most people here are not aware of this and hence they stack their discarded items in the open.

While going to offices, hospitals, relatives' houses and other places around the city, perhaps you have seen plastics, bottles, broken tins and domestic wastes lying dumped or scattered here and there beside the roads and nobody's bothering to look at them, nor is anyone coming forward to remove them to a safer place. Solving this problem without community participation is not possible.

In the premises of some police stations, we often come across seized rickshaws, taxis, discarded tyres and other such materials lying stacked in the open. During rainy season, these materials turn into breeding sources of mosquitoes. This sort of problem will never occur if such seized materials are disposed before the onset of rains. Another option to avoid the problem is to keep the things under a shed so that rainwater does not accumulate in them. But who will do this work? Are the personnel of our police stations aware? Sadly, some police stations are yet to follow this advice.

To meet people's growing need for space, construction of buildings, high-rises and shopping malls is going at a very rapid pace in many areas of the city. Unfortunately, most promoters and developers do not know how stored water at construction sites could cause harm to the society. Studies done by the entomologists of KMC have revealed that water tanks used for soaking bricks, wells, drums, pits and other water-holding places at construction sites provide ample opportunities for breeding of mosquitoes.

In some areas of Kolkata and many other cities around the country, water in many open surface drains and canals remains stagnant throughout the year and you know better whose purpose this still water actually serves. But who bothers? You must have seen how people here, including even many of our educated citizens, ruthlessly throw plastics, domestic wastes and other such materials into the drains and canals around their houses instead of dumping them in vats provided by the KMC or disposing them in a proper way. Thousands of our city-dwellers are committing this offence. I call it a criminal offence. Given the people's lack of civic sense, can the KMC people alone keep the city clean? Even the harsh critics of KMC will admit that this is not possible.

In the vast south and western parts of the city, clogged open surface drains and polluted water channels are very common and most of them have long turned into prolific breeding grounds of mosquitoes. Awareness campaigns mounted by KMC over the past several years have virtually failed to improve the situation.

Amongst us, those who have the habit of buying flowers from local markets on a regular basis must have seen water in many of them lying stored in battery shells, buckets and other containers. The florists store this water to keep flowers fresh and alive. Unfortunately, they do not change water in them regularly, as a result of which the water thus stored becomes a source of mosquitoes. Do you know what sort of mosquitoes normally breeds in them? Yes, it's the kind (*Aedes aegypti*) that spreads dengue and chikungunya.

In some hotels around Kolkata, more particularly the roadside ones, I have seen water lying stored in small masonry tanks with hundreds of mosquito larvae thriving in the water unnoticed. If the hotel owners do not clean up such water storage tanks regularly, mosquito breeding in them will continue unchecked and the people living in the neighbouring places will face the consequence.

In some areas in the eastern part of this metropolis, there are many tanneries, and most of them are non-functioning. In many of them, you will find water lying stored in masonry tanks on the ground floor or on rooftops. Mosquito breeding in such water storage tanks goes unchecked round the year. But the concerned people are not bothered.

During rainy season, the situation turns grimmer. Rainwater accumulates here and there inside the tanneries, as a result of which the number of water-holding sites increases manifold and the tanneries become a source of great danger. Most annoying, overhead water tanks in some tanneries are so awkwardly located that the mosquito control squads of KMC cannot reach them for inspection. As a result, mosquitoes keep breeding in them throughout the year. Unless owners of those tanneries become aware and cooperate with the health personnel of KMC, preventing mosquito breeding in them is literally not possible. You will be astonished to know that some tannery-owners do not even allow the KMC staff to enter their tanneries to check water storage containers for mosquito larvae.

Ponds, lakes and ditches could also become a prolific breeding ground for mosquitoes, especially when water in them turns filthy. Mosquitoes belonging to the species *Culex quinquefasciatus* mostly breed in such dirty water bodies. In some places here, I have seen ponds in which water is not only lying grossly contaminated with plastics and domestic wastes but also there is a huge growth of water hyacinth in them. And remember, *Culex quinquefasciatus* mosquito apart, *Mansonia* which spreads

Malayan filariasis (caused by a type of worm called *Brugiya malayi*) also breeds in ponds infested with water hyacinth. Since Malayan filariasis is not a public health problem in Kolkata, people here have not yet heard about this mosquito.

If we want to keep our ponds free of mosquito larvae, water hyacinth and other weeds from them have to be removed first and then the interested NGOs, persons, social organisations, local club, etc may be asked to take the ponds on lease to start pisciculture. If the concerned department of the state government accepts this suggestion and implements it, we will be benefited in two ways. First, mosquito breeding in ponds will stop for ever. Second, the government will earn some revenue from the deal.

Accumulated rainwater in a small tree-hole could also become a source of problem. But we could prevent it very easily. We just need to seal the hole with mud before the onset of rainy season. Is the job tough? No. We only need to have a good will. In many houses, rainwater lies accumulated on their rooftops for days together and the house-owners do not take any measure to remove the water. Whose purpose does this accumulated rainwater serve?

You know the answer. If people really want to solve this problem, they could easily do it simply by stirring the accumulated water with a broom.

Some people of Kolkata, like those of Chennai, store rainwater in various containers for domestic use. Some of them even keep their overhead water tanks open for rainwater to accumulate therein. This rainwater harvesting practice makes the water tanks turn into breeding sources of mosquitoes, including the malaria-bearing species called *Anopheles stephensi*. To solve the problem, shall I tell those people to stop storing rainwater? No, I will never tell them to do so because I know that in some areas of this city, water supply is still not adequate to fulfil the people's need. For them, I have only this to say: Don't stop harvesting rainwater. Store rainwater in as many containers or places as possible but please keep them tightly covered so that mosquitoes cannot enter them for procreation. Accumulated rainwater in paddy-fields is another source of danger. Mosquitoes that breed in such water spread a most dreaded disease called Japanese encephalitis (JE, in short). But we are helpless. Preventing mosquito breeding in a paddy-field is very tough. Hence we have to take only protective measures against mosquito-bites to prevent infection of the disease.

Friends, malaria, dengue and other such diseases in Kolkata will not stop tormenting us as long as we, the citizens of Kolkata, endure them. It's only the people of Kolkata who can make the city's environment completely hostile to the transmission of mosquito-borne diseases. People who blame the health department of KMC for failing to prevent an outbreak of a mosquito-borne disease need to remember that we people of the city create the environment for mosquito procreation and thus help mosquitoes spread malaria, dengue, etc among us.

The corporation alone cannot improve the situation. It's basically our collective responsibility to take care of the city. What do we need to do then? Relax! I am not going to prescribe any mammoth task to resolve it. We only need to ensure that starting from an overhead water tank to a masonry tank to a small tin can, we do properly clean every water storage container at weekly intervals and always keep our water containers tightly covered, so much so that mosquitoes do not get the chance to wing into them for laying their eggs. If we really keep our eyes open and sincerely take care of our houses, rest assured, mosquitoes are bound to stop their procreation inside our houses. And if we could really make this happen, friends, I guarantee you that malaria and dengue will soon flee from our city. And so will chikungunya. Dear fellow-citizens, as in many other cities around the world, in Kolkata too, malaria, dengue and chikungunya are all man-made problems. Mosquitoes that spread these diseases are usually borne in and around our houses.

Many patients of malaria do not complete the prescribed course of treatment, as a result of which every such patient becomes the harbinger of the parasite of the disease. Mosquitoes pick up the parasites of malaria from them along with blood-meal and then, after a certain period of time, spread them to normal people. Sadly, in spite of being repeatedly cautioned by the health personnel of KMC, people do not change this detrimental habit.

I have tried my best to make this book readable and I am sure that once you read this book, it will certainly help you gain some basic knowledge about mosquito-borne diseases and the measures you need to take to protect yourself, your family members, relatives, friends, neighbours and other people against them. Please do remember, unless you equip yourself with all the relevant information about malaria, dengue and other mosquito-borne ailments, you cannot fight against them.

We all ought to know that Kolkata has been in the grip of malaria since its inception.

Mistakes we have made so far should not be repeated. Let's wake up and start fighting together. If we remain silent, the situation will worsen in the years to come and we all will face the consequence. So, be aware and buck up!

In many badly-built, dirty and crowded houses, underground water reservoirs are commonly built below the stairs. Most of them remain uncovered. Some of the tanks are loosely covered either with a wooden slab or a porous sheet of tin or asbestos. Do you know which variety of mosquitoes generally breeds in such water reservoirs? Yes, it's the variety that spreads dengue and chikungunya. Although the mosquito control squads of KMC make periodic visits to these houses and request the house-owners to keep the reservoirs properly covered, nobody listens to them. To solve the problem, the concerned health officials of KMC sometimes plan to serve notices upon the offenders but finally abstain from taking such step in fear of being harassed by them. How bad! When will our stubborn fellow citizens rectify themselves? And when will they listen to KMC? I don't know.

And now, before I conclude, I would like to let you know that the temperature of our globe is slowly but steadily increasing. According to reports, if the global temperature continues to rise, many grave problems will crop up in near future. The polar ice caps and the glaciers will melt at a faster rate. The level of ocean will rise. Many low-lying areas around the world will be submerged. The rise in global temperature will result in drastic change in the climatic scenarios and rainfall regimes, as a result of which there will be severe drought in some areas and floods in others. The hitherto malaria-free areas of the world will turn into dens of the disease and people in millions will fall victim to the disease. Malaria apart, other mosquito-borne diseases will also start unveiling their ugly faces and people will suffer from them in greater numbers. Will our beautiful city of Kolkata remain safe then? Will our Delhi remain safe? What will happen to other cities? Will Mumbai stay safe? No. There's no way of escaping the impending impact of global warming. The entire country will suffer a lot.

So, let's stop neglecting mosquitoes. Let's all be aware and proactive. Let's all admit that mosquitoes are our Enemy No 1 and pledge to take all possible measures to prevent their procreation inside our houses, schools, colleges, hospitals and all other places around the city.

And, dear friends, if we can do this, our environment will soon become free from mosquito-borne diseases. Can't we dream for a healthy society? Can't we dream for a healthy India? Can't we dream for a healthy world?

LLIN IS MORE PROTECTIVE

Last week, my friend Manoj Raut, reporter of a Bengali Newspaper, suddenly telephoned me from the Jalpaiguri town of North Bengal and gasped, "The situation here is horrible, boss! Workers of some tea-gardens are increasingly falling into the clutches of cerebral malaria, do you know that?"

"I know, I know," I nodded. "And this is quite natural. What the hell is the district health authority doing there for mosquito control? Ask them to take appropriate preventive measures."

"Please tell me how to solve the crisis. Quick. I have to write a story."

"LLIN," I replied in brief.

"LLIN?" Manoj asked, a bit confused. "What's that?"

"It's a long-lasting insecticide-treated mosquito net. LLIN is very effective. It's more effective than our ordinary mosquito net. If you sleep under this, you will never suffer from malaria."

"Are ordinary nets not effective?'

"No."

"What!" My friend got surprised.

"Yes. Ordinary mosquito nets are not effective. They increase the risk of the infection instead."

Manoj exclaimed. "I don't believe this. You must be joking."

"No," I persisted. "I am telling you the fact."

"Who has told this?"

"Mark Young."

"Who's that?"

"He is the editor of a journal named Malaria Matters. According to him, an untreated mosquito net acts as a resting place for mosquitoes and thereby makes them sure shots when their prey emerges from the protective barrier of the net to answer the call of nature during their nighttime feeding period." By the way, have you heard the name of Dr Reuben?"

"No."

"She is a renowned entomologist of South India. She has dropped another bombshell against ordinary mosquito nets. In a paper, published in the journal NAV News Letter, Dr Reuben has written, 'Ordinary mosquito nets always drive mosquitoes to unprotected persons sleeping nearby and sometimes users too are denied protection in case holes develop in them. Contrarily, ITNs (insecticide-treated nets) not only save the people sleeping under them, but also provide a good protection for those sleeping outside.' As reported by Dr Reuben, 'In community trials with untreated mosquito nets, conducted in Thailand and some other places, reduction in the incidence of malaria couldn't be demonstrated. On the contrary, similar trials with ITNs yielded amazing results."

So saying, I insisted, "Ask the district health authorities to distribute LLINs among the tea-garden workers immediately. LLINs have no substitute. Having studied their efficacy in many experiments, experts have propounded that mosquito nets treated with a synthetic pyrethroid such as cyfluthrin (@ 50 mg/m^2), lambdacyhalothrin (@ 25 mg/m^2) or deltamethrin (@ 50 mg/m^2) could be used as an effective tool in curbing malaria and other mosquito-borne diseases."

"Can you give me a report of any specific study?"

"Of course, I can!"

"Then please tell me about the study. Name of the researcher first."

"Ok. Note it down. Li Zuzi. Chinese entomologist."

"Where did he do the study?"

"He did it in . . . in . . ." I stopped awhile and then, taking out a research paper from a file, resumed, "Yes, got it. Li Zuzi did the work in Hainan Island. It was a brilliant work. He studied the effectiveness of both treated and untreated mosquito nets."

"Results?"

"Amazing! The use of untreated nets did not significantly reduce the risk of infection, but the monthly incidence of malaria in the group of inhabitants protected with deltamethrin-impregnated nets (1.2 per 1,000 people) was much, much lower than in those protected with untreated nets(33.3 per 1,000 people) or without nets (33.4 per 1,000 people). Clearly, ordinary mosquito nets, I mean, untreated bednets cannot be the solution, especially in an endemic area. In order to improve their protective effect, we have to treat them with a synthetic pyrethroid."

"Is China using LLINs?"

"Yes. They have been using such nets since 1986, and by employing this device, they have curbed malaria by an astounding 92%. Vietnam too has got astonishing results."

Having noted all the information I provided to him, Manoj turned shaky. He whimpered, "You have really put me in a state of quandary. If I highlight only the negative points of our traditional mosquito nets, my editor will sack me from my job, understand? Please say something in favour of them so that I can save myself from being criticised by those people who have long been boasting about the effectiveness of an ordinary mosquito net."

As he stopped, I mocked, "Like other journalists of India, you have also become a prostitute. Had I been a reporter, I wouldn't have feared to speak the truth. I would have unmasked our administrators. Be brave, Guru, be brave."

My reporter friend turned serious. "No rhetoric words, boss. Give me a report only. Quick. Time is fleeting."

Disgusted, I opened a journal in haste and said, "I think this information will serve your purpose. Listen. A team of entomologists carried out a field trial with untreated mosquito nets integrated into a programme of mass drug administration from1980 to 1985 in a township of Jiangsu Province of China. Results obtained were quite interesting. The annual incidence of malaria came down from a dispiriting 18.1% in 1980 to a mere 0.045% in 1985. Similarly, in a field trial involving the students of a Kenyan school, the rate of infection of malaria dropped by 97.3% among the children who slept under mosquito nets." Having said this, I asked him, "Are you happy now, Mr Reporter?"

"Yes, yes," gushed my friend, and then, hastily saying "Old is gold, Boss, old is gold. So, ordinary mosquito net zindabad, LLIN murdabad. Ta-ta," he put down the receiver.

TALK SHOW ON MOSQUITO REPELLENTS

"Over four hundred innocent passengers were burnt alive . . . the chief minister has made an appeal to the general people to maintain peace and communal harmony in the state . . . and that concludes our bulletin, goodnight." Thus the broadcasting of the last news report from Beldanga Radio Station (BRS) came to an end. And after that, a live phone-in on science called 'Postmortem' began.

"Namaskar," Madhusudan Menon, TV anchor, began, "Dear friends, after a long one week, we are back. Today we will talk about mosquito repellents. But before we start, let me introduce our expert. Tonight we have with us in our studio the famous mosquito-man Dr Animesh Munda. Dr Munda is an entomologist, now working in the health department of BMC (Beldanga Municipal Corporation). He has done PhD on mosquitoes. He has written several books and many stories on mosquitoes. Tonight we will listen to him about mosquito repellents. Please dial toll-free 1234567890. Dr Munda will answer your queries directly."

The announcement over, Madhusudan asked, "Some experts say that anti-mosquito coils are safe and some

135

experts say that they are unsafe. Which one is right, Dr Munda?"

"The second one. Coils are harmful."

"But how do they affect us?"

"They affect us in many ways. The smoke of an anti-mosquito coil contains carbon monoxide—a highly poisonous gas whose affinity for haemoglobin (respiratory pigment) is 220-240 times higher than oxygen. Hence it combines with the respiratory pigment much faster than oxygen, thereby hampering the oxygen supply to our body cells which greatly affects the functioning of the brain, kidneys and other vital organs of our body."

"Deficiency of oxygen?"

"Yes. And hence we feel stuffy following the inhalation of the smoke."

"How are the coils made?" Madhusudan asked.

"The process is simple," Munda explained. "After extracting the insecticide pyrethrum from the petals of Chandramallika flower, the remnants of the petals are mixed with paraffin and a synthetic pyrethroid, that's all."

"By the way, some people say that the smoke of anti-mosquito coils induces cancer. Is it true?"

"Yes. Some years ago, while analysing the chemical components of the smoke of some antimosquito coils—commonly used in their country—two Australian chemists, DC Williams and ILB Henderson, detected a carcinogenic compound called diphenylamine in one of the samples tested and more annoyingly, its concentration in that smoke was much higher than in the smoke of a cigarette. So, you cannot exclude the possibility."

"Does the smoke cause any other problems?"

"Yes. Prolonged exposure to the smoke of coils can bring about a genetic change too."

Madhusudan shuddered in horror. "My God! I am sure nobody will use any coil in future after hearing this news. Anyways, let's now talk about mats. Their ingredients first . . ."

After a brief silence, Munda said, "A mat has two ingredients. One is paper pulp and the other is a chemical compound called pyrethroid. Some manufacturers mix a perfume too, to suppress the nauseating smell emitted during the burning of a mat, which camouflages the danger."

"Do coils and mats contain the same type of compound?"

"Yes."

"Are they effective?"

"No. Neither a mat nor a coil is 100% protective. The rate of protection provided by them varies from 38 to 98%. But if you sleep under a mosquito net, you will get 100% protection . . ."

Before Munda could finish, a listener called up.

"Who's speaking?" asked Madhusudan.

"Chayan Sarkhel from Dimpatty," replied the male voice at the other end. "My question is about electronic buzzers. Are they useful?"

"No," Dr Munda replied. "These are absolutely useless. In some countries, companies have been prosecuted for making claims about buzzers that they could not substantiate . . ."

"By the way," Madhusudan interrupted, "I have read in a magazine that if we take vitamin B for a long time, we will become repulsive to mosquitoes. Is it true?"

"Ridiculous bullshit!"

"Just a moment," Madhusudan cut in. "Perhaps a friend has barged in."

"Who's speaking?" he asked.

"Satarupa Sanyal from Shakuntala park," came the reply. "Is the mosquito repelling cream safe, Dr Munda?"

"No."

Madhusudan disconnected the line and said, "The business of mosquito repelling cream is thriving well around the country. What kinds of chemicals do they contain?"

"They contain many types of volatile compounds such as diethyl toluamide (deet), diethyl phthalate, diethyl methyl benzamide, N-N-diethyl benzamide, diethyl phenylacetamide, citronella oil and so on. Besides, lemon oil, cream base and scent are also present in them."

"Which one is the best?"

"Deet."

"Really?"

"Yes. Deet is the best. It is sold in the name of mylol. If you smear it on the exposed parts of your body, *Anopheles* mosquito will not bite you. But remember, it's not that much effective against *Culex* mosquito."

"Is deet safe?"

"No. Besides affecting our eyes and the mucous membrane of our mouth, deet causes many other problems such as death due to ingestion, sudden severe allergic manifestations such as rapid falling of pulse rate and blood pressure called anaphylaxis, sudden convulsion due to cerebral haemorrhage and toxic encephalopathy. One should not use this cream for a long time. However, the best way to avert the ill-effects of deet is to impregnate it into cotton items such as jackets. Anklets are an appropriate item to treat with this cream, in view of the fact that most of the biting by mosquitoes on a person who is sitting on a chair or standing, is near the ground, i.e. on the feet and lower legs," Dr Munda stopped at the interruption caused by the call of a listener from Gunrich, Gadadhar Gayen. Mr Gayen asked, "How does a mosquito repellent work, Dr Munda?"

Dr Munda thought for a while and then explained, "The mechanism varies according to the type of repellents. About coils and mats first. According to reports, after entering the body of a mosquito, the smoke of a coil or the vapour of a mat initiates adverse reactions in the mosquito's nervous system. By extending the temporary inflow of sodium ions into a nerve cell called neurone, the smoke/vapour causes an uninterrupted transmission of nerve impulses which ultimately kills the mosquito. But a mosquito repelling cream doesn't work in that way. Here the smell of the cream is important; it drives mosquitoes away by irritating their noses. Is it clear?"

"Yes, Dr Munda, thanks."

As Mr Gayen stopped, Bhajan Bhatia from Suranagar rang up. "How do DDT and malathion work, Dr Munda?" he asked.

"They work by inhibiting the action of an enzyme."

"Would you please explain?"

"Sure. Listen. As you know, the principal function of a mosquito's brain is to serve as a nerve centre receiving impulses from the receptors in the head and relaying them via the nerve cord, to effectors (which respond to external stimulus) in the posterior parts of the body. Studies have revealed that the transmission of an impulse across the junction of two nerve cells, called synapse, is a chemical reaction, catalysed by an ammonium base called acetylcholine.

"An impulse at the synapse stimulates the release of acetylcholine which diffuses across the synaptic gap and excites the post-synaptic nerve cell. The entire process is completed in only one millionth of a second and after that, acetylcholine is hydrolysed and rendered inactive by an enzyme called cholinesterase which is highly concentrated at the synapse.

"Scientists say that after entering the body of an insect, both DDT and malathion inhibit the activity of cholinesterase, as a result of which the effect of acetylcholine is prolonged and its transmission across the synapse gets facilitated. Eventually the whole nervous system of the insect gets stimulated, so much so that it suffers from convulsive contractions and dies after a few seconds . . . Do you have any other question, Mr Bhatia?"

"No."

Another caller intruded. It was Sunayani Sadhukhan, founder-leader of Jhupri Bachao Committee of Beldanga. In a husky voice, she said, "Mosquito menace in our area is terrible. What shall we do, Dr Munda?"

"Use neem oil," Dr Munda replied with a cryptic smile.

"Neem?"

"Yes."

"Is it available in the market?"

"You'll get it soon."

Sunayani turned serious. "Why are you joking, Dr Munda? Tell me something else that we can buy easily and use from today."

"Then try turmeric paste. Buy turmeric powder and mustard oil. Prepare a paste. And smear it on skin everyday after taking a bath. Mosquitoes will not disturb you."

"Shit!" Sunayani sneered. "The paste will not suit us."

Then use full-sleeved blouse and socks."

"What!" Ms Sadhukhan shot back. "Be practical, Dr Munda. We are all jhupri-dwellers."

"S-sorry," Madhusudan interrupted ingratiatingly. "Time is over, Ms Sadhukhan. So we have to stop here. But, rest assured, we will discuss this issue next week. Goodnight."

So saying, he disconnected the line and said, "Unless our general people become aware, reducing mosquito menace is very tough. Isn't it?"

"Exactly!" Dr Munda jerked. "I have been talking about this for a long time. But who bothers? Nobody understands."

"True," Madhusudan shook his head. "But don't lose heart, Dr Munda. One day our people will certainly realise this."

As Madhusudan stopped, there was another call.

Dr Munda adjusted his head-phone and asked, "Who's that?"

There was no reply.

"Who's on the line?" Dr Munda persisted.

A little later, a male voice suddenly shouted out in a manner the villain of a Hindi film does. "What's the matter, you scoundrel? Why are you talking all those bullshit sitting in the AC room? Huh? Come by the side of the canal and stay for a night with us in our shanties. All sorts of rhetoric lectures with fantastic absurdities, idiot . . . !"

Struck dumb, Madhusudan cut the line in haste, and cajoled, "Don't mind, Dr Munda. They are illiterate. But by heart they are better than us. Just take it easy."

Tick, tick, tick . . . The wall clock in the studio of the BRS went on sounding its normal rhythm. Then, following a brief commercial break began the mid-night's classical programme on Tal Betal by Pundit Rasaraj."

"N-na . . ."

MUNDA'S INPUTS FOR YOU

To trigger interests among the esteemed readers of this book, Dr Animesh Munda, entomologist of BMC (Beldanga Municipal Corporation), wants to share some important inputs about mosquitoes, etc. And these are as follows:

- A mosquito is a small (5-7 mm long), flying, blood-sucking insect. Its body is divided into three distinct parts. The fore part of the body is called head, the middle part is thorax and the last part is abdomen. A mosquito has 3 pairs of legs, 2 pairs of wings and 1 pair of compound eyes. Of the two pairs of wings, one pair helps the insect fly and the other pair of wings has been modified into the organs called halters by which the mosquito maintains the equilibrium of its body.
- Adult mosquitoes eat nectars of flowers and juices from rotting fruits.
- A mosquito larva eats bacteria, algae and other microorganisms.
- A female mosquito generally lives for a month while a male mosquito survives just for a week.

- Mosquitoes take rest preferably in dark and moist places. Their common resting places are creases of hanging clothes, cobwebs, heaps of garbage, empty drums, shoes, blades of ceiling fans, spaces between wooden furniture, etc.

- The sound of a mosquito's hum is produced by the flapping of its wings. A mosquito can flap its wings as many as 1111 times per second.

- The life cycle of a mosquito involves four stages— egg, larva, pupa and adult. Mosquitoes lay eggs in stagnant water. An egg hatches into larva. A larva develops into a pupa and from a pupa, an adult mosquito emerges. The life cycle is normally completed in 7 days.

- Mosquitoes do not breed in running water. They breed in stagnant water. Some mosquitoes breed in clean water, some in dirty water and some in both of them. Mosquitoes can breed in as little as half a centimetre of water.

- Some mosquitoes lay eggs for 5-6 times during their life-time. Some mosquitoes lay eggs for 6-8 times and some for 8-10 times. The number of eggs laid by a single mosquito at a time may vary from one hundred to four hundred.

- Among the mosquitoes, only the females bite. And they bite to get a drop of blood so needed for them to mature their eggs. If a female mosquito does not get blood, her eggs will remain immature and from such eggs, adult mosquitoes will not emerge.

- Mosquitoes that spread malaria, filariasis and Japanese encephalitis bite at night. But the dengue spreading mosquitoes bite during the daytime.

- The flying capacity of a mosquito varies from one species to another. For instance, *Anopheles minimus, Anopheles sundaicus* and *Anopheles stephensi*—all transmitters of malaria—can fly 12 km, 9 km and 2.5 km respectively. The filariasis spreading mosquito *Culex quinquefasciatus* can fly 5 km. The dengue spreading mosquitoes, *Aedes aegypti* and *Aedes albopictus*, can fly 100 m and 600 m respectively.

- Mosquitoes target their prey by smelling, not by seeing. Their noses are very powerful. A mosquito can smell its prey from a distance of 35 metres.

- An ordinary mosquito net acts as a resting place for mosquitoes and thereby makes them sure shots when their prey emerges from the protective barrier of the net to answer the call of nature during their nighttime feeding period. Besides, an ordinary mosquito net always drives mosquitoes to unprotected persons sleeping nearby and sometimes users too are denied protection in case holes develop in it. On the contrary, an insecticide-treated mosquito net not only saves the people sleeping under it, but also provides a good protection for those sleeping outside. Hence we should use insecticide-treated mosquito nets instead of ordinary mosquito nets to prevent mosquito-bites.

- Globally 350-500 million people now become infected with malaria every year and over 1 million of them die. About 90% of the global deaths occur in Africa, mostly among the children.

- Open water tanks on rooftops of hospitals, schools, colleges, high-rises, residential complexes and office buildings are great sources of the malaria-spreading mosquito in Kolkata and many other cities around India.

- Nearly half of the companions of Job Charnock, who was until recently considered to be the founder of the city of Kolkata, reportedly succumbed to malaria in just one year after their arrival in the city.

- Due to global warming and climate changes, about 8 million people in the hitherto malaria-free southern parts of North America and Europe are likely to suffer from malaria every year in near future.

- Fogging with insecticides, as done in the city of Kolkata and many other places around the country, is not a permanent solution to mosquito menace. The fog drives mosquitoes away from one area to another; it does not kill mosquitoes. The most effective means of reducing mosquito populations is to kill them at source. We just need to detect breeding sources of mosquitoes and destroy them using need-based tricks. Indiscriminate fogging yields practically nothing.

- In many areas of India, *Plasmodium falciparum* that causes dreaded malaria (cerebral malaria/

malignant malaria) has become resistant to chloroquine. Hence, cases of falciparum malaria are now being treated with ACT (Artemisinin Combined Therapy). The ACT used in the national malaria control programme in India consists of artesunate (an artemisinin derivative) and sulfadoxine-pyrimethamine. Presently, artemether plus lumifantrine fixed dose combination and blister pack of artesunate + mefloquine are also available in the country.

♦ A dengue virus contains a non-structural protein in its body which is abbreviated as NS1 (non-structural protein 1). Presence of NS1 in the blood of a patient can be detected on any day between day 2 and day 5 after the onset of fever.

The most reliable method of detecting the NS1 of a dengue virus is ELISA (Enzyme-linked Immunosorbent Assay).There is another technique called Polymerase Chain Reaction (PCR). Presence of a dengue virus in human blood can be detected by applying this technique. Besides, a number of rapid diagnostic test kits (RDTKs) are also now commercially available. By using such kits, presence of NS1 in one's blood can be detected in 15 to 23 minutes.

Most private pathological laboratories around the country are now using RDTKs at random for detection of NS1. But the problem is, the accuracy of most of these RDTKs is still not known as the results yielded by them have not yet been properly validated and hence the use of RDTKs for identifying dengue NS1 antigen has not yet been envisaged by the Directorate of National Vector Borne Disease Control Programme, Government of India—the country's only government agency to formulate strategies for prevention and control of vector-borne diseases—under the national programme for screening the cases of dengue.

One needs to remember that RDTK-yielded results concerning NS1 are not at all confirmatory for dengue. To arrive at a definite conclusion, the blood sample of an NS1 positive patient has to be tested for dengue IgM (Immunoglobulin M) antibody by Mac ELISA (IgM Antibody Capture ELISA) or ELISA after 4-5 days of the onset of fever. The use of RDTKs and the process of Immunochromatography for detection of IgM and IgG antibodies too have not yet been recommended by the Directorate of NVBDCP as reliable techniques for diagnosis of dengue.

- Mosquitoes belonging to the species *Anopheles stephensi* spread malaria in Kolkata, Delhi, Mumbai, Chennai, Bengaluru and other big cities of India. This very mosquito has long become resistant to DDT, malathion and propoxur. Hence killing this particular breed of mosquitoes by using any of these chemical insecticides is no longer feasible.

- Many people, including some qualified doctors, are still inclined to believe that *Anopheles stephensi* breeds only in clean water. This is wrong. This mosquito can breed in dirty water too.

Entomologists of Kolkata Municipal Corporation have proved this.

◆ There are 3200 species of mosquitoes around the world. These mosquitoes are broadly divided into three groups—*Anopheles, Aedes* and *Culex*.

◆ The smoke of some spurious anti-mosquito coils contains a poisonous gas called carbon monoxide and a cancer causing chemical compound called diphenylamine.

◆ Human malaria is caused by four kinds of parasites—*Plasmodium vivax, Plasmodium falciparum, Plasmodium malariae* and *Plasmodium ovale*.

◆ Like man, animals such as lizards, birds, rats, guineapigs and monkeys also suffer from malaria.

◆ Not all breeds of mosquitoes bite. There are 60 species of mosquitoes around the world which do not bite. In fact, they cannot bite, since their probosces (appendages by which mosquitoes pierce animal skin and imbibe blood) are downwardly curved and are not at all suitable for piercing animal skin. These mosquitoes are commonly called *Toxorhynchites*. The larvae of these mosquitoes devour other mosquito larvae, including the larvae of malaria, dengue, JE and filariasis spreading mosquitoes. A single *Toxorhynchites* larva can devour 25-50 larvae of another mosquito in 24 hours. This means that *Toxorhynchites* larvae are our friends, not enemies.

◆ The immature stages (i.e. eggs, larvae and pupae) of *Aedes aegypti* (the principal transmitter of dengue) are found mainly in small water containers closely associated with human-dwellings and often indoors. Hence community participation is essentially required for their destruction.

- *Aedes aegypti* females may spend their lifetime in or around the houses where they emerge as adults. This means that people, rather than the mosquitoes, rapidly spread the dengue virus within and between communities.

- The eggs of *Aedes* mosquitoes can remain viable for many months in the absence of water.

Munda's
Prescription

———

Some do's and don'ts can help conquer mosquitoes. If every fellow-citizen of this country practises them sincerely, mosquito procreation in domestic environment will certainly stop and that will help us win our yet-to-be won fight against malaria, dengue and other mosquito-borne maladies. Animesh Munda, entomologist of BMC (Beldanga Municipal Corporation), believes this by heart. And hence he has written a brief prescription for the readers of this book. The prescription contains the following do's and don'ts, which are too easy to understand, too easy to implement and too easy to communicate to others. We just need to change our mindset. Think awhile and let's all be out to bring in a healthy tomorrow.

- If you catch fever, consult a physician immediately.
- Take paracetamol to reduce fever. Don't take aspirin or ibuprofen type of medicine.
- If you want to get your blood tested for dengue NS1 antigen or dengue IgM antibody at a private pathological laboratory, then ask the concerned technician of the laboratory to do the test by ELISA (Enzyme-linked Immunosorbent Assay)

method, not by any RDTK (rapid diagnostic test kit).

*   If you want to test your blood for dengue IgM antibody, get it tested by Mac ELISA or ELISA only after 5 days of fever.

*   To know your platelet count, get your blood tested only after 4-5 days after the onset of fever. If your platelet count is between 1,50,000 and 4,00,000 per cubic millimetre of blood, you need not worry. If the count drops below 1,00,000, take advice of your physician.

*   In case you become infected with dengue, drink lots of water, fruit juice and other fluids. And take adequate bedrest.

*   Don't store water in any open container.

*   Clean masonry tanks, drums, buckets, earthen pitchers, vats, barrels and other water storage containers at weekly intervals.

*   Unused containers kept outside may be placed indoors or under a shed so that rainwater does not accumulate in them.

*   Turn your household and garden utensils (buckets, bowls and watering devices) upside down in case they are kept outdoors. This will help prevent accumulation of rainwater.

*   Ant-traps used to protect food storage cabinets can be filled with salty water instead of fresh water.

*   Ornamental pools, fountains and basement water tanks could be stuffed with guppy, tilapia or any other such larvivorous fish. Demolition of

abandoned water tanks and sealing of unused wells too are easily practicable for us.

- A small flower vase could also become a source of danger in case water in the vase remains unchanged. To make it safe, change its water at weekly intervals.

- Remove accumulated rainwater from your courtyard and rooftop.

- Do stir seepage water rigorously using a broom at weekly intervals to prevent mosquito breeding.

- Keep your underground and overhead water tanks tightly covered.

- Don't stack unused tyres in the open space.

- Remove stagnant water from construction sites or sprinkle kerosene or diesel on the water surface at weekly intervals @ 2-3 litres per 100 m^2.

- Don't stack industrial scraps, broken utensils, coconut shells, earthen teapots, jars, bottles, plastics, domestic wastes and other such discarded materials in the open space. Destroy them or keep them away from populated areas.

- Empty bitumen drums, which we often find lying indisposed after completion of road-repairing work, need to be kept upside down.

- During the season of dengue-transmission, do spray your bedrooms thoroughly with aerosols and use mosquito repellents liberally from dawn to dusk to prevent mosquito-bites. Remember, dengue spreading mosquitoes are day-biters.

- ♦ Use mosquito nets to protect babies, old people and others who may rest during the day. Such protective measure may be taken throughout the period of dengue-transmission.

MOSQUITO CONTROL IS EVERYBODY'S RESPONSIBILITY

People of Kolkata still spew venom only at the health department of Kolkata Municipal Corporation (KMC) whenever and wherever mosquito problem crops up in the city. They feel that prevention of mosquito breeding is the sole responsibility of this department. Wrong. The health department apart, some other departments of KMC—more particularly the departments of Solid Waste Management (SWM), Building, Drainage, Water Supply and Engineering—and the Public Welfare Department (PWD) and the Irrigation and Waterways Department of Government of West Bengal too need to take the buck. Let me specify here the duties of all these departments and other sectors of people with regard to prevention of mosquito procreation.

Building Department: Personnel of the building department must keep a strict vigil over under-construction buildings to ensure that wells or water storage tanks or any cesspool of water or any such accumulated water at construction sites are taken care of by the concerned promoters or developers for prevention of mosquito breeding.

In many buildings, mosquito control staff of KMC cannot reach their overhead water tanks for inspection due to the lack of a staircase. Hence mosquito breeding in them remains unchecked. This is a big problem in Kolkata. The building department needs to be serious about it. Before giving sanction to any building-plan, the department should ask promoters or developers to show staircases in their plans so that checking such water reservoirs does not become a problem in future. Amendment of the existing building by-laws by inserting a clause that getting an NOC from the health department before submitting a building-plan is a must, will certainly help solve the problem.

In case mosquito breeding is detected at any construction site or in an under-construction building, the concerned promoter/developer has to be asked to take measures to destroy mosquito larvae either by sprinkling kerosene or mobil on the water surface of water tanks/wells or by emptying them at weekly intervals. If they violate such directives, legal action (such as issuance of stop-work notices) will have to be taken against them.

Department of SWM: Old tyres are often seen lying stacked here and there in public places. During rainy season, they turn into suitable breeding sites of mosquitoes, especially the mosquitoes belonging to the dengue-bearing species *Aedes aegypti*. Hence removal of tyres to a safer place is very essential. And the department of SWM ought to do this job positively by the month of June every year, i.e. before the setting in of the monsoon. Disposal of garbage too needs to be done religiously by the department of SWM before the commencement of the rainy season. Entomologists of KMC have seen that the accumulation of rainwater in coconut shells, small plastic cups, bottles, caps of bottles, tin cans, earthen teapots, domestic wastes and other such discarded items contained in a heap of garbage greatly encourages the breeding of *Aedes aegypti*. Hence the department of SWM should undertake a city-wide cleanliness drive on a regular basis. Personnel of this department need to remember that mosquitoes can breed in as little as half-a-centimetre of water.

Drainage Department: Open surface drains clogged with waste materials are a big source of mosquitoes. Since water in such drains cannot flow, profuse breeding of mosquitoes, mostly *Culex* mosquitoes, occurs in them. Hence proper cleaning of drains is needed so that water keeps flowing down them throughout the year. But who's going to do this job? Health department? No. It's the sole responsibility of the drainage department of KMC.

Department of Water Supply: Water supply to under-construction buildings, residential apartments, colleges, office buildings, hotels, restaurants and other such places may be stopped in case the concerned people violate the antimosquito guidelines of KMC despite being repeatedly made aware by the mosquito control staff of KMC.

Engineering Department: Repairing of roads to prevent accumulation of rainwater in potholes and prompt removal of water from waterlogged areas to minimise the scope of mosquito breeding and cleaning of gully pits and catch pits to facilitate easy flow of water down the drains have to be ensured by this department for prevention of mosquito breeding.

PWD: Open surface drains, water reservoirs, overhead water tanks (OHT) in Writers' Buildings, New Secretariat Buildings, courts, medical colleges and hospitals, schools, colleges, universities, government staff quarters, office buildings, hostels and other such important structures lying in the custody of the PWD need to be monitored on a regular basis to prevent mosquito breeding in them. Regular cleaning of drains, emptying of water storage tanks at weekly intervals, keeping each and every OHT properly covered and undertaking prompt repairs in case leakage is detected in any OHT are some of the important tasks the PWD ought to do meticulously to prevent mosquito breeding in the said places.

Police Department: Weekly emptying and proper cleaning of water tanks apart, initiative to keep tyres and seized vehicles such as taxis, lorries, vans, etc under a shed has to be taken by the personnel of each and every police station across the city of Kolkata.

Kolkata Port Trust: Detection and destruction of mosquito breeding sources in Port areas of the city has to be done exclusively by the Kolkata Port Trust. Unfortunately, they don't have any effective infrastructure for mosquito control activities.

Railways Department: Necessary measures for detection and destruction of mosquito breeding sites in the premises of railway hospitals, office buildings, metro stations, staff quarters, railway workshop and other such places have to be taken by the railways department.

But how will the department do this? Does it have any entomologist? No. How shocking!

Irrigation and Waterways Department: Some portions of the Beliaghata Canal, Tolly's Nullah and other sewerage canals have long become heavily clogged with water hyacinth, dirt and various kinds of waste materials, as a result of which mosquito breeding, mostly the breeding of *Culex* mosquitoes, in those places is going unchecked. And the people living in nearby wards are the worst sufferers. Mosquito control workers of KMC, who have since March 2011 been meticulously doing larvicidal spray in other portions of these canals using small rowing-boats as transport, cannot take any measure to destroy mosquito larvae in those clogged portions of the canals simply because of their inaccessibility. Unless cleaning operation is done by the department of irrigation and waterways of Government of West Bengal, solving such problem by KMC is literally not feasible.

School Authorities: Cleanliness drive by mobilising students may be undertaken inside the school premises once a week under the supervision of a teacher, especially during the rainy season. If done religiously, this will help prevent mosquito breeding. To increase students' awareness about mosquito breeding sources, a short interactive discussion between students and a teacher of life science in every school once a month would be very effective.

Tyre Retreading Centres: Tyres should be kept under a shed to prevent accumulation of rainwater in them. Unfortunately, owners of the tyre retreading centres in Kolkata are least bothered about it. They stack tyres in the open space. During rainy season, huge breeding of mosquitoes occurs in them and the people living in the nearby areas face the music.

Promoters/Developers: At construction sites, mosquito breeding in plastic drums could be checked by keeping them properly covered. Water tanks used for soaking bricks and other construction purposes may be emptied at a weekly interval by using pumps. Done, this will help prevent mosquito procreation.

Ward Councillors: Fogging is a puerile exercise. Hence we need to stop it immediately. As per the guidelines of the Directorate of the National Vector Borne Disease Control Programme, Government of India, source reduction remains the only means of achieving mosquito control in urban areas. Ward councillors of KMC need to ensure that such national anti-mosquito guidelines are strictly implemented in their wards by the vector control staff of KMC. Ward councillors are more acceptable to the people living in their constituencies than the officials of KMC. People, especially the voters, hardly ignore the advices of their leaders. Hence they could easily make people take the simple measures to prevent mosquito breeding in and around their houses.

Role of Ministers: Mosquito control activities so needed to prevent transmission of malaria, dengue and other mosquito-borne diseases must run under the guidance and supervision of qualified entomologists. Regrettably, people of the medical fraternity having no or very little knowledge of the subject have traditionally been planning and implementing mosquito control strategies in different districts of the state. For reasons best known to them, the higher officials of the state health department have not yet taken any initiative to deploy entomologists in different districts of the state. Municipalities and Municipal Corporations (except Kolkata Municipal Corporation) too are running without entomologists. Improving such a sorry state of infrastructure is very tough unless our Honourable Health Minister and the Minister of Municipal Affairs and Urban Development personally look into the issue. If our ministers remain silent, nobody else will do this job.

Health Department of KMC: Undertaking source elimination drive is the first and foremost job that has to be done by this department on a regular basis. While inspecting human-dwellings, market places, under-construction buildings and other construction sites, medical colleges and hospitals, educational institutions, workshops, garages, office buildings and other such places, mosquito control staff of the department need to check each and every water-holding container or site for mosquito larvae and take need-based measures to destroy them at once. Containers needed to be checked at various places are listed in Table 1. Prompt larvicidal spray in all those large water-holding containers or sites that cannot be emptied or managed by the general people too has to be done by them.

Prompt issuance of legal notices and filing of cases in the Municipal Court against people such as private house-owners, promoters, owners of tyre retreading centres and many others is another task that the health department of KMC has to accomplish meticulously whenever and wherever any event of violation of the antimosquito guidelines of KMC occurs.

These apart, undertaking mass awareness campaigns, studying mosquito behaviour, measuring larval densities of disease-spreading mosquitoes on a regular basis directly come under the purview of the health department of KMC and hence the department has to act accordingly.

Duties of the Citizens: By employing some common-sense approaches, citizens of Kolkata can easily prevent mosquito breeding in and around their houses. For example, unused containers kept outside may be placed indoors or under a shed so that rainwater does not accumulate in them. Household and garden utensils (buckets, bowls and watering devices) kept outdoors may be turned upside down when not in use to prevent accumulation of rainwater. Ant-traps used to protect food storage cabinets can be filled with salty water instead of fresh water. Ornamental pools, fountains and basement water tanks could be stuffed with guppy, tilapia or any other such larvivorous fish. Demolition of abandoned water tanks and sealing of unused wells too are easily practicable.

Masonry tanks are fertile breeding grounds of *Aedes aegypti*. Hence these water storage tanks ought to be emptied and scrubbed at weekly intervals. Scrubbing of the inner walls of a masonry tank is needed because if this is not done, the eggs of *Aedes aegypti*, that can withstand desiccation for a period of more than one year, will remain glued to its inner surfaces and begin to hatch as soon as the tank is refilled with water.

Small water storage containers such as plastic or iron drums, buckets, earthen vats, earthen pitchers, earthen barrels, empty battery shells and tin cans too become the breeding sources of mosquitoes if we keep them open and do not change their water at weekly intervals. If we keep these water containers covered with tight lids or screen, mosquitoes will not breed in them.

In many houses, rainwater accumulates on their courtyards and rooftops. To prevent mosquito breeding in such places, we just need to stir the accumulated rainwater with a broom.

In some poorly-built houses, underground water reservoirs are commonly found located below stairs and most of them remain uncovered. Huge breeding of mosquitoes, especially the mosquitoes belonging to the dengue-bearing species *Aedes aegypti*, occurs in these reservoirs throughout the year. To solve the problem, we need not spray any insecticide in them. We just need to cover them with lids.

Broken utensils, coconut shells, earthen teapots, jars, bottles, plastics, domestic wastes and other such discarded materials also create problem if they are stacked or thrown in the open space. Consequent upon the accumulation of rainwater in them, they turn into mosquito breeding sites. If we destroy these unwanted materials or keep them away from our locality, there will be no problem.

Table 1: Checklist for detection of mosquito larvae in an urban area

Where to check	What to check
Human-dwellings	Masonry tanks, small water storage containers (such as earthen pitchers, vats, barrels, flower pots, drums, etc), basement water tanks, underground water reservoirs, overhead water tanks, seepage water beneath overhead water tanks, flower vases, discarded items (glass, tin, iron, plastic, coconut shells, domestic wastes, etc), artificial fountains, open surface drains, uncovered septic tanks, unused bathtubs, cisterns, accumulated water on courtyard or any other place in and around the house, etc.
Workshops and garages	Water tanks, discarded tyres, empty battery shells, accumulated rainwater in scraps lying stacked or scattered in the open space, etc.
Under-construction buildings and other construction sites	Water tanks used for soaking bricks and other construction purposes, wells, drums, lift-wells, accumulated water on basement, empty bitumen drums, mixers, etc.

Schools, colleges, universities, medical colleges, hospitals, office buildings, housing complexes, etc	Water storage tanks, overhead water tanks, open surface drains, etc.
Market places	Water storage containers, especially water-holding battery shells at flower shops; coconut shells, accumulated rainwater in heaps of garbage, etc.
Police stations	Water storage tanks, overhead water tanks, heaps of seized materials such as rickshaws, lorries, tyres, four-wheelers, etc.

A LEADER'S FIGHT AGAINST MOSQUITOES

In spite of having funds crunch, political conflicts and many other constraints, the municipal corporation of an unplanned overcrowded city can achieve a lot in terms of containment of mosquito-borne diseases provided a modest proactive political leader sits atop the corporation's health department and honestly gets involved in planning and implementing strategies needed to fight against such ailments. Atin Ghosh, a noted leader of Trinamool Congress Party, has set an instance which one may consider as an eye-opener for other political leaders around the country. As a ward councillor of KMC (Kolkata Municipal Corporation), Atin Ghosh has been winning the civic election for more than two and half a decade past. And needless to say, he works for people relentlessly.

In the framework where mosquito control has traditionally been considered a trivial task, Mr Ghosh has stood against the detrimental flow, conceived various prolific measures and made the health department of KMC implement them to change the dispiriting scenarios of malaria and dengue in the city of Kolkata, besides resorting to many other unprecedented steps to improve the basic health care facilities provided by KMC. This political man, to me, is a trend-setter. Over the past three-and-half years, he has been steering almost all health-related activities of KMC with clockwork efficiency. The job, which was supposed to be done by the controlling health officials of KMC, has been done by a non-medical man.

Situated by the side of the River Hooghly, the city of Kolkata sprawls over an area of 206.2 square kilometres and it is inhabited by over 4.5 million people. The area of KMC is divided into 15 boroughs consisting of a total of 144 wards. The city's daily floating population is around 6 million. There are 1500 registered slum clusters and nearly 39% (1.8 million) of the city's population are slum-dwellers.

Malaria and dengue are the two age-old public health problems in this metropolis. Providing primary health care facilities apart, activities with regard to prevention and control of mosquito-borne diseases are carried out exclusively by the health department of KMC.

Mr Ghosh is not an entomologist. Still he has aptly realised that curbing mosquito-borne diseases without mosquito control is just not feasible. And presumably this self-realisation warranted him to consider mosquito abatement a top priority. He took over the charge of the health department of KMC as a member of the mayor-in-council (MMIC) in June 2010 and gave a free-hand to the entomologists of his department to monitor mosquito control activities to combat malaria and dengue in the 'city of joy'.

In order to undertake emergency control measures and cross-check the activities of mosquito control workers in different wards of KMC, Mr Ghosh has constituted twenty-one Rapid Action Teams (RATs) comprising a total of 160 agency-provided trained field workers. Six of them are working as the Central RATs and the rest fifteen teams as Borough RATs (@ 1 RAT per borough) comprising six field workers each. Mobility support by hiring a vehicle at Rs 800 to Rs 1000 per day too has been provided to each RAT at his behest.

The RATs are all doing their job most religiously. The main activities of a Central RAT include: 1. Periodic inspection of under-construction buildings and other construction sites, market places, hospitals, schools, colleges, university campuses, office buildings, sky-scrapers and other such important places for elimination of breeding sources of malaria and dengue spreading mosquitoes under the direct guidance of entomologists. 2. Undertaking emergency mosquito control measures to prevent transmission of malaria and dengue. 3. Cross-checking the activities of Borough RATs and the mosquito control staff working in different wards of KMC. 4. Helping the department undertake surveillance as and when required for collecting information about breeding sources of the city's malaria and dengue-bearing mosquitoes—*Anopheles stephensi* and *Aedes aegypti* respectively.

Like the Central RATs, Borough RATs are also doing very important job and the activities of a Borough RAT are: 1. Making surprise visits to cross-check mosquito control activities of field workers in different wards of the borough. 2. Undertaking contingency measures for prevention of dengue and malaria. 3. Providing assistance to consultant entomologists in collecting inputs with regard to the prevalence of mosquito breeding sites as per the format prescribed by the department.

The idea of building an impartial in-house monitoring system for mosquito control by forming Central and Borough RATS is the brainchild of Mr Ghosh and this idea is absolutely new in India.

In 2011, Mr Ghosh set up a small Mosquito Research Laboratory to facilitate research on mosquitoes of Kolkata. Health officials of the country need to realise that for planning need-based scientific strategies against malaria and dengue, precise information about the breeds of mosquitoes involved in their transmission is very essential and collecting such information is possible only when you are having research facilities at your disposal. By establishing the Mosquito Research Laboratory, Mr Ghosh has done a brilliant job and one may consider this as an eye-opener for all concerned. According to Dr PL Joshi, former director of the Directorate of National Vector Borne Disease Control Programme (NVBDCP), Government of India, the Mosquito Research Laboratory of KMC is a first-of-its kind laboratory in eastern India. Entomologists of the Directorate of NVBDCP have said that by establishing such laboratory, Atin Ghosh has ushered in a new era of mosquito control activities in the city of Kolkata which the other civic bodies of the country can accept as a model.

As an employee of the health department of KMC, I feel immensely delighted and honoured when the health department of the Government of West Bengal and other non-KMC organisations of the state of West Bengal send their staff to our Mosquito Research Laboratory to get them trained on mosquito control. Even the harsh critics will be surprised to know that following the establishment of this laboratory, undertaking research on city's mosquitoes has become quite easy for the entomologists of KMC. People who tend to undermine the research activities of KMC, may please note that the entomologists of KMC have in the past three years got their research papers published in three medical journals of international repute such as the Transactions of the Royal Society of Tropical Medicine and Hygiene, Dengue Bulletin (published by the World Health Organization) and Journal of Vector Borne Diseases (published by the Indian Council of Medical Research).

Some unprecedented infrastructural changes too have been made by Mr Ghosh to step up mosquito control activities in different wards of KMC. In February-March of 2013, mosquito control responsibilities were assigned to dedicated non-medical staff. Selection of the staff was done from among the permanent employees of the department and the suitability of a staff was judged by his efficiency, not by his designation. One staff at ward level and one staff at borough level were chosen for steering mosquito control activities as a Ward Vector Control In-charge (WVCI) and Borough Vector Control In-charge (Br VCI) respectively. Thus 15 BrVCIs and 144 WVCIs were selected for running the KMC-sponsored mosquito-bashing programme across the city of Kolkata.

Since March 2013, the Br VCIs and WVCIs have been working under the technical guidance of the consultant entomologists. Tasks assigned to a WVCI are: A. Collecting information from the malaria clinic located in his ward on a daily basis for undertaking vector control measures on an urgent basis. B. Maintaining ready-stock of insecticides and equipment throughout the year. C. Meeting the ward councillor twice a week for apprising him of the ongoing vector control programme in his ward. D. Ensuring that the work diaries of field workers working in his ward are signed by the ward councillor or his/her representative on a daily basis.

Activities of a Br VCI are: A. Visiting one ward every day to check mosquito control activities of field workers in the ward. B. Overseeing day-to-day activities of the Br RAT. C. Mobilising the Br RAT for undertaking emergency mosquito control measures soon after the receipt of a report/news concerning the occurrence of malaria or dengue anywhere under his borough. D. Looking after the repairs of knapsack sprayers and fogging machines in different wards of his borough. E. Providing assistance to entomologists in conducting surveillance as and when required.

In Kolkata, uncovered overhead water tanks, seepage water, water tanks built for soaking bricks and other construction purposes, unused wells, abandoned water tanks, deserted fountains, water for curing newly-built rooftops, basement water tanks and other such water-holding sites act as the main breeding sources of the city's prime malaria-bearing mosquito *Anopheles stephensi*, specially during the winter season, and these breeding sources are called Mother Foci of the mosquito. According to entomologists, the best way of controlling *Anopheles stephensi* population in this city is elimination of its Mother Foci from the city's environment. After holding series of talks with the entomologists of the department, Mr Ghosh asked his department to start mounting a city-wide drive for detection and destruction of the breeding sources of this very mosquito right from the beginning of the year. The health department of KMC has been doing the job accordingly.

Practising physicians of Kolkata know very little about the national guidelines on treatment and management of cases of mosquito-borne diseases. To make them aware, Mr Ghosh organised a workshop on 13 January 2013 where experts from the Directorate of NVBDCP explained the treatment and management procedures for dealing with the patients of complicated malaria and the fatal version of dengue in details. Around 400 doctors from around the city attended the workshop.

This apart, another workshop involving ward councillors and ward medical officers of KMC was organised by Mr Ghosh on 14 January 2013. National guidelines on mosquito control were elaborately discussed in the workshop by resource persons from the Directorate of NVBDCP. The main reason for organising such workshop was to trigger interests among the ward councillors about mosquito control, besides making them realise that without their active support, the fight against mosquitoes and mosquito-borne diseases in their wards could not be won by the mosquito control staff of KMC alone.

In the field of mass awareness-raising campaigns through leaflets, Atin Ghosh has brought in a phenomenal change. Prior to his joining KMC as the MMIC (Health), the health department used to print unattractive monolingual leaflets—all in black and white—to disseminate information about the do's and don'ts for prevention of malaria, dengue, etc. Mosquito control staff of the department used to distribute those leaflets among the city-people at random.

People whose mother tongue was English could not read the leaflets printed in Bengali. Similarly, Bengali-knowing people could not read the leaflets printed in English. Mr Ghosh thought about this issue quite seriously and asked his department to prepare multicoloured leaflets each containing the same messages printed in four different languages—English, Bengali, Hindi and Urdu. And the department did it accordingly. Multilingual leaflets helped people from every sector understand the KMC's messages quite easily. This initiative was new in the history of KMC and it was immensely appreciated by numerous people around the city. In all fifteen lakh leaflets were distributed in 2010-2012 @ five lakh leaflets per year. Through the leaflets, these three important antimalaria messages, each printed in the chronological order of Bengali, Hindi, Urdu and English languages under the caption "Mosquito is bearer of diseases. Three tips for survival", were disseminated to the people: 1. If you suddenly catch fever, get your blood tested immediately. Malaria clinics of KMC are located very near to your residence. 2. Don't store water in any open container. 3. Use mosquito nets.

School students constitute the most sensitive part of our society. Hence their awareness about mosquitoes and mosquito-borne diseases is very essential. Having realised this, Mr Ghosh caused to publish three lakh twenty-five thousand multicoloured booklets in four different languages (Bengali, English, Hindi and Urdu) and distribute the booklets among the students of as many as 701 schools of the city. Neither any civic body nor any state health authority around the country has brought out such colourful booklets for school students ever before.

To increase people's awareness, a music audio CD and a video CD containing a Bengali song on prevention of mosquito-borne diseases were prepared by KMC in 2010 and that too was caused to be done by Mr Ghosh. Since 2010, the KMC has been playing the music audio CD on-air through various FM channels and the video CD on 9-11 TV channels for one-two months every year. Such high-voltage campaign has never been launched by the health department of KMC before.

In May 2013, the KMC prepared two documentary films on prevention and control of malaria and dengue, one for increasing people's awareness and one to help mosquito control workers of the department learn about various techniques of destroying mosquito larvae with or without using insecticides. And again the idea of preparing such DVDs was conceived by Mr Ghosh. From 1 August 2013, the health department of KMC showed the mass educative documentary film (of 18-minute duration) to the people of Kolkata from 2 pm to 10 pm on all seven days of the week by using two publicity vans each fitted with a mobile LED Digital Screen (7.5 ft x 5.5 ft). The campaign continued till the middle of October 2013, involving a monthly cost of Rs. 4,80,000 (@ Rs. 8,000 per day per van). Neither the medical fraternity of KMC nor any political leader of this civic body has ever thought of doing such thing before.

In June 2013, three lakh booklets on prevention of mosquito-borne diseases—175000 in Bengali, 75000 in Hindi and 50000 in Urdu—were brought out by the health department of KMC at the behest of Mr Ghosh. What the common people should do to prevent mosquito breeding and mosquito-bites, what they should do in case they catch sudden fever and what they should do after being diagnosed as patients of dengue or malaria have been told in the booklet in a very lucid manner. Addresses of all malaria clinics and dengue detection centres of KMC and the names of 15 borough executive health officers together with their cellphone numbers have also been mentioned herein. These booklets were handed over to all the ward councillors of KMC for distribution among the distinguished fellow-citizens of Kolkata. People, including the political leaders of the opposition party, have profusely appreciated this initiative of Mr Ghosh.

The electricity consumption bill issued by the Calcutta Electric Supply Corporation (CESC) too was used by the health department for disseminating educative messages at the behest of Mr Ghosh. As part of their Corporate Social Responsibility, the CESC authorities sent out these three messages of KMC under the title 'Dengue-Malaria Alert by Kolkata Municipal Corporation' for people's awareness: 1. Malaria and dengue-spreading mosquitoes breed in stagnant water. Don't let water stagnate anywhere. 2. Free facilities for diagnosis of malaria and dengue are available at your nearby health centre of KMC. 3. Never go for testing of dengue by Rapid Diagnostic Test Kit. ELISA is the only recommended method. As many as five lakh consumers received these messages in August and September 2013 through their bills sent by the CESC for consumption of electricity in July and August 2013 respectively. The idea of campaigning through electricity bills is quite interesting. Other municipal authorities in India may like to resort to this noble technique to spread awareness among the people about malaria, dengue, etc.

During June-August 2013, altogether 750 multicoloured hoardings (8 ft x 6 ft) containing do's and don'ts for prevention and control of malaria and dengue were put up at the busy intersections of the city. This apart, 15000 educative banners were put up in different wards of KMC. Additional 5000 banners were put up at different important places such as housing complexes, medical colleges, hospitals, nursing homes, office buildings, cinema halls, schools, colleges, universities and market places. At Durga Puja pandals too, 5000 multicoloured banners were put up in October 2013 for people's awareness. Publicity campaign through such huge number of hoardings and banners has never been mounted by KMC before.

Awareness-raising meeting involving the concerned ward councillor and the local people too was organised in each and every ward of KMC. And again, Mr Ghosh is the man who conceived and implemented this plan by mobilising his department. During March-August 2013, about 500 such meetings (@3-4 meetings per ward) were organised in KMC area. Many people were benefited by this campaign.

Blood-tests done at a private pathological laboratory for detection of dengue NS1 antigen and dengue IgM antibody are indeed very expensive and there are many people in Kolkata who cannot afford to bear the expenses of such tests. Atin Ghosh realised this problem and set up five dengue detection centres in KMC area in 2011 to help the poor city-people get their blood tested for dengue free of cost. Blood samples from suspected patients of dengue are being collected at different malaria clinics of KMC (138 in all) and brought in to these dengue detection centres for diagnosis of the disease by a most reliable method called ELISA (Enzyme-linked Immunosorbent Assay). The Directorate of NVBDCP has profusely appreciated Mr Ghosh for establishing such charitable dengue detection centres.

The menace of *Culex* mosquitoes in many places around the city of Kolkata worsens in February-March every year. And the main breeding sources of this pesky winged lady are the sewerage canals. Water in these canals is highly polluted and it remains stagnant throughout the year. Hence breeding of *Culex* mosquitoes occurs in them more or less throughout the year. Since the canal-edges, where *Culex* larvae are found in greater numbers, are inaccessible to spraymen, they cannot treat those places with a larvicide. In March 2011, finding no other suitable alternative to deal with the problem, Mr Ghosh prescribed the use of small rowing-boats as transport to undertake larvicidal spray in all the highly mosquitogenic sewerage canals of the city to destroy the larvae of *Culex* mosquitoes. The plan has worked wonders and people have appreciated this initiative.

Three to 4 months after becoming the MMIC (Health) of KMC, Mr Ghosh proposed to ply speedboats along the city's two main polluted canals—Beliaghata Canal and Tolly's Nullah—to prevent breeding of of *Culex* mosquitoes. Initially, some critics, including a section of journalists, for reasons best known to them, ridiculed his proposition pleading that the plan was pompous and it would fall flat. But Mr Ghosh did not react to them. He remained unfazed and asked his department to undertake the study. To implement his idea, the department hired four speedboats, at a cost of $US 59.1 per boat per day (inclusive of the drivers' daily wages). Two boats plied the Beliaghata Canal and two Tolly's Nullah, at 8-15 nautical miles per hour for 4-5 hours daily for six days a week from November 2010 to April 2012. The effort worked wonders. Speedboat-generated waves resulted in substantial decline in the densities of egg rafts, larvae and pupae of *Culex* mosquito in both canals. The results obtained during November 2010 to October 2011 were published in the Transactions of the Royal Society of Tropical Medicine and Hygiene in 2013 (volume 107). As a most unconventional ecofriendly approach to mosquito control, the work gained ground in the city and got a wide publicity through media.

Under-construction buildings in Kolkata provide ample opportunities to mosquito procreation. Since construction work goes almost throughout the year, breeding of mosquitoes, including the city's malaria and dengue-bearing mosquitoes (*Anopheles stephensi* and *Aedes aegypti* respectively) occurs there perennially. But who bothers? Despite being repeatedly requested by the mosquito control workers of KMC, the concerned promoters or developers do not take any measure on their own to prevent mosquito breeding. In May 2013, Mr Ghosh found out an answer to this problem. He caused the civic authorities to pass a resolution that the health department would carry out larvicidal spray in under-construction buildings on a regular basis, incurring expenses from the promoters/developers @ Rs. 2.5-3 per square metre for one round of larvicidal spray. Thus he has opened up an avenue for his department to earn revenues by selling its larvicidal service to non-KMC organisations around the city. As an entomologist, I consider this a historic decision and I salute the MMIC (Health) of KMC, I mean, Atin Ghosh, with warm regards for conceiving and implementing it. Has any political man in KMC tried this before him? No.

On every Friday, Mr Ghosh holds meeting with chief municipal health officer (CMHO), deputy CMHOs, borough executive health officers, entomologists and all other concerned officials of the health department to review the progress of mosquito-borne disease control activities going in different wards of KMC. In a bid to step up mosquito control activities in each ward of KMC, Mr Ghosh personally visited all the 15 boroughs of KMC separately and spent 3-5 hours in each borough holding talks with the ward councillors, ward MOs, Ward VCIs and Borough VCI of the borough. Such meetings were held during May to August 2013. This sort of meeting has never been held in KMC before.

Achievements: A new era of mosquito control activities needed to prevent mosquito-borne diseases has begun in Kolkata under the stewardship of the MMIC (Health), Atin Ghosh. Field workers and other mosquito control staff of KMC, who were once not at all conversant with the techniques of identifying mosquito larvae, can now do the job quite easily. Selecting need-based measures for destroying mosquito larvae too is no longer a big problem for them.

Collecting information from fields regarding the prevalence of the larvae of malaria and dengue-bearing mosquitoes using prescribed formats has become a regular phenomenon in each and every ward of KMC. Population densities of *Anopheles stephensi* and *Aedes aegypti* (transmitters of malaria and dengue respectively) in different high-risk wards are now monitored by the consultant entomologists on a regular basis by calculating the larval indices of these mosquitoes. Studying susceptibility status of mosquito larvae to various insecticides has also become very easy following the establishment of the Mosquito Research Laboratory.

In each ward of KMC, day-to-day activities of mosquito control workers are now kept recorded in a register as per the format prepared by entomologists in accordance with the instructions of Mr Ghosh. The inputs are recorded under these heads: A. Date . . . B. Ward No . . . C. Road/Street/Avenue/Lane visited . . . D. Number of houses checked . . . E. Number of water containers checked for mosquito larvae . . . F. Number of water containers found positive for the larvae of the dengue spreading mosquito *Aedes aegypti* with addresses . . . G. Number of water containers found positive for the larvae of the city's malaria-bearing mosquito *Anopheles stephensi* with addresses . . . H. Number of water containers found positive for the larvae of the city's nuisance mosquito *Culex quinquefasciatus* with addresses . . . and I. Action taken (larvicidal spray/source reduction/release of guppy fish/issuance of legal notice). As far as my knowledge goes, no other municipal corporation or state health department in India keeps mosquito-related information in this manner. Borough RATs and Central RATs too keep their daily findings recorded in registers as per the formats prepared by entomologists.

Going by the published reports, transmission of malaria in Kolkata City has been going since its inception. Nearly 50% of the 1200 companions of a British Merchant Job Charnock, who was until recently considered to be the founder of this city, reportedly succumbed to malaria in a span of only one year after their landing in the city way back in 1690.

Until the mid-1950s, the ravages caused by this disease were unremitting and indeed terrible. Then with the implementation of the National Malaria Eradication Programme (NMEP) based on indoor residual spray with DDT, much relief followed. Unfortunately, in the mid-1970s, as in many other parts of India, in Kolkata too, malaria swayed back into the scenario and its incidence, more particularly the cases of falciparum malaria (dreaded version of the disease), started spriralling. Going by the official statistics, the average annual incidence of falciparum malaria was 0.09% (1/1404) in the 1970s. It rose to 4.1% in the 1980s (610/14707). And in the 1990s, the figure shot up to a staggering 18.5% (7820/42118).

In 1995, besides 18 other cities of India, Kolkata too was declared as a high-risk malarious city by the Directorate of NVBDCP (erstwhile NMEP). Officially, 52 people died of falciparum malaria in this city during that year. In 1996-1997, the emergence of a chloroquine-resistant strain of *Plasmodium falciparum* (causative agent of cerebral/malignant malaria) in the city was revealed by a study done by a team of experts from the Directorate General of Health Services under the Ministry of Health and Family Welfare, Government of India. Unfortunately, the health department of KMC somehow missed to take note of it. Years passed by. Treatment of *P. falciparum* cases with chloroquine continued through all the malaria clinics run by KMC. The practising physicians of the city too did not stop treating their patients of falciparum malaria with chloroquine. Resultantly, 318 city-dwellers died of falciparum malaria during 1996 to 2010: seventeen in 1996, thirty-eight in 1997, fifty-three in 1998, sixty-three in 1999, fifty-five in 2000, twenty-nine in 2001, twenty-eight in 2002, six in 2003, nineteen in 2004, three in 2005, one in 2006, four in 2008, one in 2009 and one in 2010.

In 2009, the health department of KMC tried to obtain ACT (Artemisinin Combined Therapy) from the Directorate of NVBDCP, but failed for some corrigible technical impediments. The concerned officials of the state health department too did not help the KMC get ACT from the Central Government. Finding no other alternative, the health department of KMC procured ACT from the local market and started using it through some of its malaria clinics. But the religious use of ACT in treating cases of falciparum malaria through each and every malaria clinic of KMC began only after Mr Ghosh became the MMIC (Health) of KMC. Incidentally, Mr Ghosh himself had to stay admitted at a nursing home for a couple of days for treatment after being afflicted with falciparum malaria about 15 years back. Possibly this was the main reason why he took up the issue of malaria abatement as a major challenge in his career.

For implementing the National Policy on treatment of falciparum malaria at all city-based government hospitals and nursing homes too, Mr Ghosh intervened. He wrote letters to the health authorities of both the Government of India and the Government of West Bengal urging them to ensure that patients of falciparum malaria are treated with ACT at all non-KMC health establishments across the city. His initiative yielded results. Some erring doctors at government-run hospitals, who were in the habit of treating falciparum malaria with chloroquine, changed their mindset and started using ACT. Atin Ghosh's endeavour thus helped prevent transmission of chloroquine-resistant *P. falciparum* among the people of Kolkata.

The efforts of Mr Ghosh have reaped splendid harvests. Malaria scenario in Kolkata has improved phenomenally. In 2010, altogether 355293 febrile patients visited the KMC-run clinics to get their blood tested for malaria. Blood samples drawn from these patients were examined by microscopy. Of them, 96693 samples proved positive for malaria. The rate of transmission of malaria, expressed in terms of slide positivity rate (SPR), was

27.2%. Falciparum malaria comprised 14.7% (14226) of the total number of positive cases.

In 2011, the number of malaria cases in the city came down to 41642 (SPR-17.5%), of which only 4200 were the cases of falciparum malaria. In 2012, there was a further decline in the number of malaria cases. The slide positivity rate came down to 9.3% (32659 cases out of 350147 blood samples tested). And the number of *P. falciparum* cases was only 3403. In 2010, one person died of complicated falciparum malaria in the city. But in 2011 and 2012, there was no death here due to malaria. The scenario has shown further improvement in 2013 (15856 malaria cases till 17 November, including only 902 Pf cases with no death).

The multipronged strategy of the health department of KMC against mosquitoes and mosquito-borne diseases, that has been going in the city of Kolkata since June 2010 at the behest of Mr Ghosh, has, to say the least, brought in a sparkling success and lapped up commendable appraisal from the World Health Organization. In an alert issued to travellers through its International Travel and Health Bulletin in March 2012, the World Health Health Organization said: "Risk of falciparum malaria and drug resistance in Kolkata is relatively lower than the other places of the state of West Bengal."

Pertinently, mosquito control activities in different districts of the state of West Bengal have for aeons been going on under the administrative control of doctors who, I am sorry to say, by and large know very little about the subject. Tangible initiative to recruit qualified entomologists so needed to plan and implement strategies for mosquito control has not been taken yet. Mr Ghosh has shown a path which the controlling officials of the state health department ought to opt to walk down to improve the infrastructure, which currently is in tatters.

The achievement in terms of prevention and control of dengue too has been outstanding. Over 1850 confirmed cases of dengue were reported from this metropolis during 2012. But this year, till 20 November, only 162 cases of dengue were reported from here. Last year, two persons succumbed to dengue in this city. This year, no death has occurred here so far. Hopefully, the dengue scenario in the city will remain well under control.

The member of the mayor-in-council (Health) of Kolkata Municipal Corporation, Atin Ghosh, has shown a path which the other state health departments of the country ought to opt to walk down to step up mosquito control activities for prevention and control of malaria, dengue, chikungunya and other diseases spread by mosquitoes. Atin Ghosh has proved that a proactive political leader can do a lot in terms of prevention of mosquito-borne diseases.

I would like to mention here that I don't have any intention of having a crack at the medical fraternity of India but the true scenario has to be brought to surface somehow or the other.

EYE OF A MOSQUITO COUNSELLOR

It was around 9 o'clock in the morning. Sitting alone in the dark interior of a discarded shoe beside a clogged open surface drain in the northern part of the city of Beldanga, Mayabati, a young hump-backed pregnant lady belonging to the city's nuisance creating community *Culex* Quinquefasciatus, was crying with madness. Suddenly, her mother, Leelamoyee, dropped in.

"Why are you crying, Maya?" Leela asked, gently rubbing her daughter's swollen tummy with her proboscis. "What's happened, my child?"

After a brief silence, Maya sobbed, "That bastard has come to poison my labour room. I can't lay eggs there. It's just impossible. My children (read larvae) won't survive."

Leela turned curious. "Who are you talking about, Maya?"

Instead of giving an answer, Maya said, "Let's get out of here, Mom, and see yourself."

Leela and Maya came outside the shoe.

A young mosquito control worker of Beldanga Municipal Corporation (BMC) carrying a knapsack sprayer in his back was chewing guthkha standing beside the drain. Thousands of mosquito larvae were wriggling therein. Maya drew attention of her mother, pointing to the worker with her proboscis, and said, "The rogue is here with an ill motive. He will poison the drain."

Leela watched the BMC employee and burst out with laughter. "Silly girl! He is not a killer. He is a genuine friend of our community. Just wait and see how he fights a pseudo battle to protect our kids. This man is against Jagannath Panja . . ."

"Jagannath?" Maya asked curiously. "Who's that, Mom?"

"Don't you know?" Leela asked, moving her eyes vigorously.

"No, Mom."

"Update your knowledge-base, Maya," Leela admonished. "This is needed for your own safety. Anyways, listen. Jagannath Panja is the member of the mayor-in-council (Health) of BMC. He is sly and cunning. Since 2010, he has been continuously provoking the employees of the health department of BMC to kill us at source. Chief municipal health officer (CMHO) Dr Nirjan Baker, entomologist Dr Animesh Munda and some other personnel of the health department of BMC have flared up at his provocation. But God is there. Some employees are not listening to him. Politically they are against Jagannath. And they are out to botch up Jagannath Panja's antimosquito policy . . ." Leela paused here for a while and then, glancing at the spray-man near the drain, whispered to her daughter, "Look at there, Maya. Watch the show he runs."

The spray-man of BMC put the knapsack sprayer on the ground, detached something from the tip of its hose in promptness and again took out the sprayer in his back.

"What has he detached, Mom?" Maya asked.

"SWIRL plate," Leela answered, smile-faced. "He will now spray a poison called Temephos and the poison will come out of that machine and he will finish his work very soon and flee from here."

Leela's prediction came true. The spray-man finished his job in 5 minutes and disappeared from the place.

A cold shiver ran across the face of Maya. "What will happen now, Mom? No one will survive there . . ."

Leela smiled cryptically and then went back to the retiring room along with Maya and spent the day sitting there almost idle. After the sunset, they winged out and landed up near the drain.

"Look at the water inside. How many of them have died?" Leela asked.

Having made a quick check, Maya said, "20-25%, Mom."

"Right. The figure cannot be more than this."

"But how is this possible, Mom? Was the poison not that effective?"

"No. It's not the question of the poison's effectiveness. The way you sprinkle this particular poison on water surface matters. Remember, Temephos is an organophosphorous compound. This is a contact poison, which means that if our kids come in contact with this chemical, they will die. According to the World Health Organization, this is a sheer poison . . ."

Having said this, Leela stopped for a while and then, after giving a hug to her daughter with her two forelegs, continued, "The spray-man of BMC did a great favour for our kids. He sprinkled the poison without using the SWIRL plate, as a result of which Temephos came out through the nozzle in a jet, which could not cover the surface of water in that drain uniformly. Temephos reached only some portion of the water body. The other portion remained uncontaminated and hence most of our children escaped the danger. Maya, insecticidal spray without using a SWIRL plate is useless. There are many workers in BMC who do not use SWIRL plate sincerely despite being repeatedly warned by Jagannath Panja not to commit such blunder."

"Why don't they use the SWIRL plate?" Maya asked. "Please explain, Mom. I need to know about this."

"Listen," Leela explained. "If one sprays the poison using a SWIRL plate, the stream of the poison will come out through the nozzle in the form of a cone @ 760 millilitres per minute. If one does the spray without using a SWIRL plate, the rate of discharge of the poison will be 3-4 times more. And the stock of the poison will be exhausted soon. Which one is better for the people unwilling to spend time for BMC? Take the poison in a container, finish it as quick as you can, kill your duty hours doing this and that for your own welfare and come back to office. By escaping their own duties, they have long been paving the way for our kids to survive in drains, roadside gullies, abandoned water tanks, ponds, basement water tanks, masonry tanks, unused wells, ditches, accumulated waters at construction sites and many other such labour rooms around Beldanga. Jagannath Panja alone cannot change the rotten work culture of Beldanga Municipal Corporation. So, relax, my child, and keep spawning there. Good time is coming for us. Beldanga will be our city very soon . . ."

Hriday and Madhu

Barrelling her way through the crowd of patients, a tiny winged mother, her daughter, Madhu Stephensi (female *Anopheles stephensi*, city's malaria-bearing species), in tow, entered the doctor's chambers and exhorted, "Doctor, you have to save my child!"

A rotund Dr Hriday Stephensi smiled. "Do sit down." His multiple eyes had already made an assessment of the daughter. "Very nice," he thought to himself. "Still a virgin."

Madhu sat by her mother and having noticed his eyes noted how greedy he must be.

"What's the problem?" asked Hriday.

"She's lost her appetite, Doctor," the mother wailed. "And she's now even stopped talking to her friends. In fact, she's been behaving quite abnormally of late."

Hriday rose, approached the young thing and solicitously applied pressure to her abdomen. "No," he announced, "it's not dyspepsia. Must be something else. Could you enlighten me a little further?"

"Why, yes, Doctor," the old one offered. "She shows no signs of even wanting to mate. She's afraid she never will become a mother."

"And might you be aware of any reason for that?"

"No, Sir," she replied. And then after a brief pause, continued, "I can't bear to see her in this misery, Doctor. You've got to help!"

"Now, now, my dear. Don't worry, I have just the cure for her." Still looking at the mother, he sat beside Madhu and confided, "You'll have to leave us alone. What I have to tell her is of a professional nature."

"But of course, Doctor."

By now the moist indoor air had caused Madhu to perspire. "Why this self-limiting decision, Madhu?" murmured Hriday, eyeing her closely.

No reply.

"Madhu, Madhu, Madhu, come out with the truth. Time is fleeting," he cajoled.

Finding no way out of her dilemma, Madhu said shakily, "I'm terribly afraid, Sir."

"Of what? Madhu, tell me everything."

"Yes," Madhu acquiesced. "It was that report in the newspapers the other day. The member of the mayor-in-council (Health) of Beldanga Municipal Corporation (BMC), Jagannath Panja, said that those who dared ignore the BMC directives and supported our procreation in their houses would be taken to task. Doctors of the health department of BMC would sue them. Sir, if they carry out this massacre, where will I lay my eggs? It's better I desist from mating than dream uselessly of becoming a mother." Tears streamed down Madhu's cheek.

"Silly, silly girl," Hriday laughed. "I saw that bit of news, too. Ridiculous bullshit, all those paper clippings. Read between the lines and you'll soon look through all their gimmicks. They've been raving and ranting on about the same thing for the past several years but how many would you say have been punished for doing exactly what has been banned? No one. People here aren't afraid of their threats. Be a darling, Madhu, and forget all about that. Enjoy life. It only comes once!"

Still sceptical and no less confused, Madhu replied, "Do you know what happened the other day? The owner of the house where we've lived for aeons suffered a mad fit and began to empty all his containers of water, in the process killing all our sprightly children in a jiffy. Sitting in that dark store-room, I watched the massacre in tearless grief. You can't imagine how painful it was!" Her entire being convulsed and she wept copiously. "Even as I watched, I came to know that the neighbours had done the same thing in their houses. I was shattered. I still am."

"Stop this at once," hissed Hriday. "I've yet to come across a girl as foolish as you. Who must you imagine yourself to be? Life isn't so cut and dried, dear. If you want to survive, be led by your head, not your heart."

Still in shock, Madhu sobbed, "What must I do, Sir?"

"For one, tell me, what is your flying capacity?"

"I don't know, Sir."

"Bah! Is there nothing you know about yourself?" He glowered at her. "Well, let me be the judge. Yours is 0.8 to 2.5 kilometres. Do you know what that means?"

She thought awhile and said, "I don't understand, Sir. Honestly, I'm beginning to feel quite nervous here."

"A most illiterate thing," Hriday grumbled.

"If you scold me any further, Sir, I'll collapse," Madhu groaned. "Already I'm getting palpitations."

Hriday cooled perceptibly. "Sweetheart, what I mean is that within a radius of 0.8 to 2.5 kilometres you can spawn anywhere. And I don't think you'll find it a problem finding a small site in such a big area where there is even a little water. Madhu, realise your own power. Don't fall victim to baseless fear. Be active and learn to scramble. If you kill time sitting around depressed, our community is going to suffer a lot."

Now Madhu understood. "May I leave now, Sir?"

His cunning eyes flashed in anger. "Selfish girl, how can I let you off so easily without collecting dakshina?" The polygamous bastard that he was, Hriday's evergreen mind throbbed with outrageous emotions in a preparation to devour nectar from the flower that was blooming before him. "Madhu, don't be cruel. Look at me. Try to realise how I am breaking inside."

Puzzled, Madhu gaped at him.

"Come, my heart, sit on my lap. Please, I am going mad."

Madhu recoiled in disgust. "How could that be possible, Sir? You are too old to satisfy me . . . you're like my father, isn't it, Sir!"

"How wrong you are, Madhu. I may be aged but I'm not impotent. And remember, we don't believe in sexual restrictions. Indeed, we're a step ahead of the most liberal Homo sapiens. Our custom is: Baba apon Ma par, tar meyeke biye kar, sujog peley makeo dhar (Father mates with mother, then the daughter, get the chance, fuck your mother, too)."

Madhu dropped her eyes in surrender and silence shrouded them. Hriday embraced her and brushed his thick elongated hairy mouth against her abdomen. A hot flame ran through Madhu's blood and the two became one, plunged into heavenly bliss.

Minutes passed. "It's brilliant, Sir, I mean Hriday, Babumashai."

"Indeed, eh!"

"Are you happy now?" asked Madhu coyly. "Am I free to leave?"

"Yes, yes, of course," he told her sharply. "But remember, save for a very few intrinsically panic-prone, backboneless creatures, as is your landlord, the people of Beldanga are all genotypically magnanimous. They don't flare up against any provocation on our members. Unbelievable! Similarly, the field workers of BMC— only three to four for each BMC ward—are no less broadminded. Seemingly dull-headed, they are all very sly and, save for one or two, they never hesitate to betray one another to save our children."

Noticing Madhu's surprise, he explained, "Yes, it's true. Unless compelled by circumstantial pressures, they don't raid homes to kill our offspring. Literally unskilled and habitually lazy, they are governed by the pleas of the people's representatives and other VIPs who, in fact, know nothing about our community. Most of the times, they remain busy fulfilling their own selfish ends. Is that not a boon for us, Madhu?"

"Yes," she agreed. "I too know something about their support and have a lot of respect for them. But my mother says the BMC commanders deputed to monitor the fight against our community are ruthless. She says they are all big doctors and if they want they can easily wipe us out. I'm really scared of them, Hriday."

Hriday laughed. "That, too, is a rumour, darling. Your mother might have heard this from others. Actually some people here are very jealous. They are trying to break the friendship between the BMC doctors and our members. The truth is, they're all damn nice. They come late and leave early. They spend their time in office discussing issues of the world, including the deterioration of work culture across the country, especially among government employees. Since they don't know the basics of our population dynamics, they never really bother about actually fighting against us.

"Some idiots often complain that the doctors of BMC are worthless, that they come to the office only to collect their additional profits—Rs 35,000 to Rs 75,000 each per month—without even rendering minimal service. However, I'm not at all bothered about it. Why? Because the health authorities of BMC, including the chief municipal health officer, thanks to a patented style of functioning, never misunderstand their doctors. Besides, where else would you find civic authorities who, despite being aware that the BMC doctors are incapable of steering the fight against us, insist they carry on instead of appointing professional killers (read entomologists)? Remember, too, that the leaders of all political parties in the city of Beldanga are hand in glove. After all, it's a doctors' lobby. Traditionally, the BMC authorities worship them as diamonds of society and currently a whopping amount of over Rs 5 crores is being spent per annum just to pay their emoluments. Where else in this country would you find such profligacy in the name of protection? You won't, Madhu.

"Many people, including newsmen, are inclined to believe that the BMC commanders are waging the war efficiently. But I know the wastage of ammunition. Imagine, Madhu, what the outcome might have been had this war been waged against us by anybody but these doctors! These BMC doctors are an excellent lot, our friends in disguise. So don't be afraid of them and exhort your friends not to knuckle under any of their threats."

Madhu felt the adrenaline pumping through her. Overwhelmed by her metamorphosis, she bowed, kissed Hriday goodnight and winged out of his chambers.

In the darkened outer room she looked around for her mother and got the aroma she had only recently been familiarised with. "Yes, there she is." The old lady was being serviced by a rapacious juvenile partner. "Given our freedom, Beldanga will be ours very soon," Madhu chuckled. Suddenly she felt needle-like probes (probosces) digging at her bust and lower body. Contemptuously, she jerked free and flew into the future, chuckling to the disappointed Romeos in her wake, "Too late, idiots, the great Hriday beat you to it!"

DEAF BUREAUCRACY

Despite being repeatedly requested by the concerned mosquito control squads of BMC (Beldanga Municipal Corporation), the superintendent of a very well-known government-run hospital in the eastern part of the city of Beldanga had not taken any corrective measure to prevent mosquito breeding in the premises of the hospital. The situation was grim. As many as 44 water tanks were lying there uncovered and nobody was bothering to cover the tanks. Both malaria and dengue spreading mosquitoes were breeding in them peacefully. There were 12-13 open surface drains and all of them were brimming with mosquito larvae. Besides, there were 10-12 open pits in front of the emergency ward, staff quarters, each harbouring mosquito larvae over the years. The health department of BMC had issued a legal notice to the hospital authorities twice to take measures. But that effort too misfired.

On 28 May 2013, Animesh Munda, entomologist of BMC, wrote a letter to Shakil Ahmed (IAS), municipal commissioner (MC), explaining the sorry state of the hospital. The letter reached him through Dr Nirjan Baker, chief municipal health officer (CMHO), and Jagannath Panja, member of the mayor-in-council (MMIC) of the corporation's health department.

Shakil Ahmed is a health-conscious hyperactive officer. "Demolish the Everest in a minute or empty the Bay of Bengal in a day" is his policy. Sky is his limit. Mr Ahmed is so intelligent and honest at his duty that for collecting a petty reporting format or any trivial copy of a government circular—that one can easily manage to bring in through e-mail—he can send anyone from his office to any place in the country by a flight spending thousands of rupees from the exchequer of BMC. Earlier, he was a branded supporter of Proletariat Protection Front of India. But now he is a different persona. Like many other IAS (Indian Administrative Service) officials of the Fighters' Mansion, he has also undergone a sudden metamorphosis. And yes, Shakil is now a branded loyalist of the Hon'ble chief minister of the state of Jhautala. If the state CM asks him to run one-and-half-a-kilometre at a stretch, he will run ten-and-half-a-kilometre. The controlling officials of different departments of BMC by and large consider him the latest edition of Mohammad Bin Tughlaq and they are now praying for his transfer from the Black Building.

Munda's letter took a long 20 days to reach the table of the MC from the office of the MMIC (Health). It was in the humid afternoon of 19 June 2013. After going through the Munda's note, Shakil Ahmed called up the CMHO. Despite being a patient of sever cardiac ailment, Dr Baker ran to the chamber of Mr Ahmed and quite smilingly got from him the order for drafting a letter of request to the secretary of the public works department (PWD), Government of Jhautala, for an early solution to the problem brought in by Munda.

With his heart beating hardly for 50-52 times per minute, Dr Baker came back to his chamber almost running and sat before his computer to prepare the menu ordered by the MC. He did the job religiously keeping all other official job aside. The letter to be dispatched to an IAS officer under the signature of Shakil Ahmed read, "Sir . . . The mosquito control squads of our health department are frequently coming across various mosquitogenic sites inside the premises of different government-run hospitals located in BMC area . . . The prevailing conditions require immediate improvement to ensure stoppage of mosquito breeding therein. Initiatives for regular cleaning of drains and other such mosquito breeding sources, if resorted to by the PWD, will indeed be of immense help in making the premises of our hospitals unconducive to mosquito procreation. I would request you to cause necessary intervention for making this feasible, etc."

The food cooked by Dr Baker was served to Shakil. And Shakil took the dish from Dr Baker, ate it and said, "Nice, Dr Baker."

Dr Baker is a dedicated employee. Unlike his deputy CMHO & OSD (Health) Dr Koutilya Makal, Dr Baker has an extramarital relationship with BMC. The eyes of his wife require an urgent surgical operation. But who bothers? He has no time to get the thing done for his wife. Working for BMC is always considered by him as an elixir of his life. Koutilya utters the name of his wife 3-4 times everyday sitting by Nirjan. But he learns no lesson from Koutilya. Nirjan bothers about the health of Koutilya's wife, he prescribes medicines for her at the request of Koutilya. But the wife of Dr Baker has not yet been offered the scope of having her opthalmic problem highlighted at least once by his husband in front of Koutilya. Since 4 July 2013, Shakil Ahmed has been closely watching this easy-to-hook soldier of BMC. Like some other foxy people of BMC, he too has learned how to gain fame and popularity at the cost of Dr Baker's flesh and blood. A man who serves BMC authorities forgetting about the welfare of his family is a rare specimen. And all are well aware of this.

In the late evening of 19 June 2013, after signing the letter, Shakil asked Dr Baker to fax the letter. Dr Baker shook his head and did.

Munda got the news and muttered to himself, "The people concerned will now work. There will be no mosquito breeding in and around the hospital . . . An IAS officer cannot ignore the request of another IAS officer . . . Our commissioner has indeed done a brilliant job!"

On 25 July 2013, a mosquito control worker handed over a letter to Munda. Written by the concerned mosquito control supervisor, the letter read, "Sir . . . No sign of improvement is in sight yet. Mosquito larvae are wriggling everywhere. The situation has remained the same . . ."

Munda's face turned pale. He phoned Dr Baker and said in a dismal voice, "What the hell are you doing sitting in your chamber, Nirjanda? Don't waste your time drafting letters for our MC. Stop asking us to work for the BMC. If the IAS officers do not work, why should we? Stop sending letters to them. Look at yourself. Look back at your family. They need you. They need your presence and service. And remember, I won't walk down the path you have shown . . ."

"Tomorrow, we will discuss about this issue . . ." So saying, the meek voice disappeared from the line.

LESSONS FROM
A LEADER OF
MOSQUITOES

It was late in the evening. In her dark, dank den in South Beldanga, the winged matriarch crossed and uncrossed her speckled legs, killing time with the accomplices she held sway over. Suddenly, some juvenile females of Beldanga's dengue spreading community *Aedes Aegypti* winged in and bumped into her. She fixed them with a look of consternation.

"Sorry, Madam, very sorry," they gasped.

"Well, all right," she responded. And then, rolling her multifaceted kidney-shaped eyes, she asked, "Why the agitation? What's the problem?"

"It's terrible, ma'am, we had a narrow escape," they replied with a shudder. "You see, we were relaxing in a public urinal with our boyfriends. We were all sprawled out on a nicely made cobweb when two hoodlums in a black van suddenly appeared. They stopped awhile, smoked their cigarettes and then, glancing furtively this way and that, they ran down the main road firing continuously from their big American gun. Terrible gun, this was. The busy street grew foggy in the twinkling of an eye. Passers-by fled, pinching their noses. Roadside inhabitants slammed their doors and windows shut. Some of the gas entered our restroom and made it stuffy. What an experience! We won't ever forget it!"

The venerable queen and her ladies remained unfazed. One of them remarked, "Nothing is unknown to us. You need not say any more. But tell us, how many of you died of it?"

"None," one juvenile volunteered. "But it would certainly have killed us had we not acted in such haste. Thank God, we somehow managed to leave the place."

Eliciting no response, the young one's resentment began to become apparent and, looking at the leader, she asked, "Who are they, Didi? And when will they come again?"

"Don't worry. Just relax and listen," the leader said. "Girls," she continued, "the persons you saw firing are not hoodlums but employees of the Beldanga Municipal Corporation (BMC). However, remember, they are our good friends. Don't misunderstand them. It is with their tacit support that we have not faced any problem yet in the city." She sighed in recall of a recently-taken photograph and continued, "Yes, it's mist, not fog. Contrary to popular belief, it only repels us instead of killing us. Death occurs only when someone is trapped directly in a closed room with no means of escape. Earlier they used to play this game once or twice a year in a ward of the city. Now they do it quite frequently, more precisely at bi-monthly intervals. Still, I can guarantee you will never see them again for the rest of your life of only a month's duration."

So saying, she looked outside, muttered to herself, and then resumed, "Given the emergence of every new generation at a minimum of ten days' interval, your sixth or seventh filial generation will next get a chance to witness this wonderful show. It's merely a pseudo battle which the BMC people have been waging for more than twenty years against our community simply to hide their real embarrassment from being unable to annihilate us by killing our kids in aquatic environments across the metropolis."

The juveniles looked at one another in astonishment. The leader understood their curiosity and explained, "It may sound strange, but it's true. The fogging is a puerile exercise."

Her audience fairly buzzed with the humour of the situation. "How much do they spend for this misfiring, Didi?" one juvenile asked.

"Several lakhs a year," Didi replied.

A bit fogged, another juvenile asked, "If it doesn't work, then why don't they stop it, ma'am?"

"Silly girl," Didi shot back. "Don't use anti-community expressions. Will you be happy if they stop this practice and launch a real war against us? Instead, pray to God it never stops!"

"Sorry, Didi," the young one said, ashamed.

"Well," the leader went on, "our learned local enemies—hardly four or five, including the doctorate bastard of the BMC—have tried several times to ban the practice but failed because of the strong opposition by the political leaders of Beldanga who are, incidentally, our best friends. Since they come to power on the verdict of the electors, they always patronise fogging and other such hollow activities to prove their efficiency or else they apprehend that no one will vote for them the next time. Where will you find such a congenial environment in this country?"

Looking at an associate, the leader urged, "I have said enough. I need to rest. But do please tell them the nicest part of the story. They ought to know that, too. But keep the voices down for no outsider should know. It's highly confidential."

One of her cohorts rose and started speaking, "Dear friends, all this is about how the BMC people save our community and lose their own dignity. Some scoundrels, especially those who wish us dead, blame the doctors of BMC for wasting public funds by asking the BMC's Supply Department to procure such fogging machines in the name of destroying us. They are absolutely mistaken. Profits gained from the trade, we know, are no doubt very big but, mind you, our honest employees of the Supply Department of BMC never expend their dividends on whims. Instead, they deposit these in their own accounts. Being part of the public, tell me, are they committing any crime? We at least do not think so. Those who consider them thieves need to swallow this quinine-coated truth and stop spewing hogwash. And that concludes my bulletin."

Delighted with her clarification, the juveniles buzzed past in single file to kiss the speaker on her needle-like mouth to express their admiration. The speaker revelled in her importance and then took her seat.

Before Didi could dismiss them from her presence, one juvenile asked in a shaky voice, "I'm still somewhat confused. Will you please help me, Didi?"

"Sure. What's your problem?"

"You see," said the young one, "it happened yesterday. Around 11 in the morning some people came to a police barracks and fired some shells indoors on orders from a local leader and the officer in-charge of the police station. The fog soon dissipated and none of us was affected. Sitting in a discarded tyre outdoors, barely 25 metres from the battlefield, I saw, tight-lipped. I was so scared that I couldn't leave my hideout for a moment until late evening. I'm still annoyed, Didi."

"Don't be," Didi advised. Looking around, she added, "That, too, is a great hoax. Listen, though the BMC employees use the prescribed missile P2 (read pyrethrum 2% extract), the attempt yields practically nothing. Let me explain. As per the norms, if anybody complains about the attack of DEN-V (Dengue virus) missile, at least 50 houses surrounding the household of the victim—having a total indoor space of 5,100 cubic metres—have to be treated thoroughly and the work, say our enemies, must be accomplished prior to our departure from the bedrooms, preferably before 9 o'clock in the morning. Interestingly, the BMC people never do this. They are like the cops of Beldanga. The moment they arrive at a spot and start firing indoors, it's already two-three hours late. The consequence: they waste money, sweat and blood indoors, and we enjoy the drama resting outdoors. Let them feel smug in their assumed importance. We know better, so don't bother about it."

Much relieved, the juvenile bowed to the leader. "Thank you, Didi."

"Didi, zindabad . . . zindabad . . ." some overenthusiastic compatriots started shouting, whirling around their revered Didi.

"Stop this nonsense. Don't be so silly. You are our future, be serious and think of your fellow citizens!" Didi lambasted them. "You need not leave us tonight. Stay here and enjoy. See how undisturbed my hostess, a maid, and her three school drop-out daughters are sleeping on that torn mattress, completely at our mercy. Let's make a meal of them, they won't mind."

It was an invitation that brooked no repetition. So they all joyfully tucked in, with the deathly still night the only eyewitness. How appropriate!

ENTOMOLOGISTS CAN GIVE IT A CRACK

Having all my previous efforts miserably failed to get the departmental need fulfilled, one day, possibly in the first week of June 2009, I personally met Alapan Bandyopadhyay (IAS), municipal commissioner of Kolkata Municipal Corporation (KMC), and urged him, "Sir, would you please deploy at least three qualified entomologists for my assistance? I am overburdened. In a city like Kolkata's sprawl, overseeing mosquito control activities by me, a lone entomologist in the department, is just not possible. Please do me a favour, Sir. After a brief silence, he said he would try.

And yes, he tried and he did it. He spoke to the then Hon'ble city mayor, Bikashranjan Bhattacharya, and got his nod. In a week's time, a resolution was passed in the meeting of the mayor-in-council for an early engagement of three entomologists on a contractual basis. Accordingly, three consultant entomologists were deployed on 1 July 2009. And I heaved a sigh of relief. Together with the three consultant entomologists, 25-30 medical officers too were engaged by the health department of KMC on a contractual basis.

Following the instructions of the mayor and municipal commissioner, the monthly remuneration for each consultant entomologist was fixed at par with that of a medical officer, i.e. Rs. 15,000/. I will commit a great mistake if I do not admit here that like many other doctors of the department, the then member of the mayor-in-council (Health) of KMC (a medical man by profession) too was quite reluctant to deploy entomologists in KMC. A proposal initiated by me in this regard had been outright rebuffed by him. And this came to me as a terrible shock and I was demoralised, so much so that I decided to quit KMC in protest. The timely help of the mayor and municipal commissioner made me change my decision and I started working for the department along with three consultant entomologists.

But the arrival of three entomologists in the health department was not welcomed by the medical fraternity of KMC. Doctors, who had long been projecting themselves as well-wishers of mine, became my enemies overnight. They began contradicting me and my colleagues on trivial issues. Detrimental efforts to ridicule our activities started pouring in from a section of erratic medical officers. Some of the doctors were out to undermine the posts of consultant entomologists. Some of them stopped rendering cooperation to them during their inspection in different wards. To my discontent and utter disbelief, a clear line of demarcation between entomologists and the doctors of KMC came to surface, which was very frustrating.

In the late 2010, a team of 5 medical officers of the department jointly wrote a letter of contempt to the member of the mayor-in-council (Health) of KMC, Atin

Ghosh, pleading that the official rank of a consultant entomologist cannot be considered equal to a medical officer (MO) by any stretch of imagination. Hence the monthly remuneration of an MO ought to be put above that of an entomologist. When I came to know about this dirty letter, my eyes welled up with tears. A sense of helplessness gripped my mind. Still I did not give any reaction to this remark. I only told my colleagues to prove their indispensability for the department. And they started doing it most religiously. Atin Ghosh stepped in and overruled the doctors' evil objection.

In this context, I need to mention the name of another bureaucrat of KMC (Tapas Chowdhury, WBCS) who had very aptly realised the need of entomologists for running the fight against mosquitoes in right direction. He believed that the work load of an entomologist was no less than that of an MO. Hence he urged the civic authorities to keep the monthly remuneration of a consultant entomologist always similar to that of an MO whenever the issue of hiking monthly remuneration of an entomologist came up for a discussion in the meeting of the mayor-in-council of KMC.

Needless to mention, entomologists of KMC are rendering their service relentlessly. And there is no denying the fact that a new era of entomological activities so needed to begin a real fight against mosquito-borne diseases has begun in the city following the deployment of three consultant entomologists in the health department of KMC. Apart from establishing the basic laboratory facilities needed to impart training to the concerned staff of the department on mosquito control, the KMC has gathered many interesting information about the malaria and dengue spreading mosquitoes of Kolkata from the studies done by the entomologists. Some notable findings are here:

Anopheles stephensi breeds more in rainwater than in chlorinated water: In Kolkata, the main transmitter of malaria is *Anopheles stephensi*. This mosquito breeds more in rainwater collections than in the KMC-supplied chlorinated water stored by people in a variety of containers. During July to September 2009, larvae of *Anopheles stephensi* were detected in as many as 60 types of water containers across the city and surprisingly, over 90% of those containers were found to contain rainwater while the rest of the containers were filled with chlorinated water. Findings of the study were published in the Journal of Vector Borne Diseases in 2012 (a journal brought out by the Indian Council of Medical Research). Based on these findings, the health department of KMC now gives more emphasis on inspection of rainwater accumulations for destruction of the larvae of *Anopheles stephensi* every year during the rainy season and the times thereafter.

Anopheles stephensi procreates in filthy water too: On 13 July 2009, filthy rainwater collection in an abandoned handcart on the premises of an office building of KMC was found brimming with anopheline larvae. On 23 July 2009, anopheline larvae were detected in muddy water in a pit by the side of a tramline. On 7 August 2009, such larvae were found in two discarded drums on the courtyard of an old dilapidated house. On 12 September 2009, presence of such larvae was noticed in a small abandoned water tank; water in the tank was filthy, blackish and highly contaminated with dead algae. On 22 September 2009, profuse breeding of anopheline larvae was detected in a masonry tank at a construction site. Water in the tank was dirty and heavily contaminated with algal bloom. Samples of mosquito larvae were collected from all these sites by the consultant entomologists, brought to the mosquito research laboratory and reared in mosquito cages till the emergence of adults. Surprisingly, the adults emerged from the larvae were all found to be of the breed *Anopheles stephensi*. This was a very serious finding and it helped the department plan strategies against this mosquito to prevent transmission of malaria in the city.

Aedes aegypti in Kolkata commonly breeds in masonry tanks, tyres, drums, etc: Field studies conducted by my entomological team have revealed that the dengue-bearing mosquito *Aedes aegypti* in this city breeds mostly in masonry tanks, discarded tyres, drums and other small domestic water storage containers. To prevent transmission of dengue and chikungunya in Kolkata, we need to disseminate this information to our city-dwellers together with an advice to empty each and every water container at weekly intervals. The department of solid waste management of KMC too is required to take steps with regard to the removal of unused tyres or their proper storage by the owners.

Construction sites are a big source of danger: Larvae of *Anopheles stephensi* are found in greater numbers at construction sites. This clearly suggests that the mosquito control squads of KMC ought to give more emphasis on inspection of under-construction buildings and other construction sites across the city for detection and destruction of *Anopheles stephensi* larvae.

During the monsoon and the times thereafter, the rooftops of under-construction buildings and other such structures in Kolkata turn into fertile breeding grounds for mosquitoes, mostly of the breed *Anopheles stephensi*. This too was found out by our entomologists. The field workers and other concerned staff of mosquito control were not aware of this and hence they would not check such places. They used to check water holding places/sites/containers only on the ground floors while making house-to-house checks in different wards of the city for mosquito larvae. They have changed their practice. They now inspect rooftops too for mosquito larvae.

Predicting an impending outbreak of dengue is now possible: Consultant entomologists of KMC calculate the larval indices of *Aedes aegypti* (i.e. House Index, Container Index and Breteau Index) in different wards of the KMC meticulously in every month from January to December every year. And based on the calculated indices and some other parameters, they predict an impending episode of dengue in the city. In 2012, one such prediction was made by a consultant entomologist. Sadly, the concerned mosquito control staff did not bother to listen and hence the disease broke out in some areas of the city in July; transmission of the disease continued till December 2012, involving more than 1800 cases and two deaths.

According to experts, if the Breteau Index of *Aedes aegypti* (i.e. number of water containers positive for *Aedes aegypti* larvae per 100 houses) in an area is 50 or more, the risk of transmission of dengue in the area would be high while the risk of transmission of the disease would be low if the index remains 5 or less.

Mosquitoes born in the adjoining buildings of a slum spread malaria among the slum-dwellers: On 27 August 2009, a larval surveillance was conducted in a slum on 47 Chakraberia Road (south) in ward 72 following the receipt of a report concerning the occurrence of some cases of malaria among the slum-dwellers. The entomological search that had been undertaken in the affected slum yielded no larvae of *Anopheles stephensi*. Larvae of this mosquito were found at the adjacent under-construction building on 45/2 Chakraberia Road (south). Antimalaria strategy for the slum was planned accordingly and the department got results shortly. Similarly, transmission of malaria in a slum on 37/4 Dr Suresh Sarkar Road in ward 59 of KMC was prevented by destroying the *Anopheles stephensi* larvae in an adjoining under-construction building. So was the story of achievement in another slum on 4A Rakhal Das Auddy Road in ward 82 after the destruction of *Anopheles stephensi* larvae on the rooftop of the nearby office building of a government-run press on 32 Gobinda Auddy Lane. Again, on 22 September 2009, huge larval breeding of *Anopheles stephensi* was detected in an under-construction building on 26 Dilkhusa Street and one house on 4A Radhagobinda Saha Lane in ward 64. These two breeding sources of *Anopheles stephensi* were found to be the prime underlying reason for continued transmission of malaria among the people living in the nearby slums. The situation turned comfortable soon after the destruction of mosquito breeding sites in the premises of those two houses. Clearly, entomologists can do a lot to improve the quality of mosquito control activities. Without entomologists, mosquito control is not possible. All concerned need to remember this.

DEVASTATING 1997

The scar of the day is still very fresh in his mind. And there's none in the health department of Beldanga Municipal Corporation (BMC) with whom Dr Animesh Munda can share his pains and pathos. The 52-year-old man still sheds hot tears while walking down a busy street alone, remembering the day of ruination of his professional career.

After joining the mosquito control department (MCD) of BMC back in 1989 as the BMC's one and only entomologist, Animesh Munda began working for his department with immense passion, like a lunatic. He was the second officer in his department, the first being a deputy chief municipal health officer (Dy CMHO). Since the MCD was a wing of the health department of BMC, the administrative control of the department was laid entirely in the hands of Dr Gourhari Ghosh, chief municipal health officer (CMHO) of BMC.

For a period of long 10 years—1990 to 2000—there was no member of the mayor-in-council (MMIC) to steer activities of the health department. The mayor of BMC, Sushanta Chatterjee, used to look after the health department himself by collecting information from the CMHO, Dr Gourhari Ghosh. Otherwise a dedicated Marxist leader belonging to the Proletariat Protection

Front of India (PPFI), the mayor had, in fact, no time to spare for discussing each and every issue of the health department. And, quite obviously, Gourhari became the undeclared policy-maker of his department. Dr Ghosh used to take decision on all grave issues himself and managed to get them duly ratified by the mayor. Nobody had the guts to question his credibility. By cashing in on his own political links with some high-profile leaders at the headquarters of PPFI, Gourhari became the undeclared MMIC (Health) of BMC. The deputy CMHO, who was the in-charge of the MCD, was a mere puppet of Gourhari.

There were 22 branch offices under the MCD. Mosquito control activities across the city of Beldanga would run through these offices under the technical guidance of Munda. Since the office hours of all branch offices of the MCD were from 8 am to 2 pm, Munda would leave his home between 7.30 and 8 in the morning and make surprise visits to 2-3 branch offices on every working day of the week. He used to check staff attendance, monitor activities of mosquito control workers in fields and impart in-field training to them on how to detect and destroy mosquito breeding sources using various techniques. To review mosquito control activities in different parts of the city, he used to convene meeting with all supervisory staff at weekly intervals. Since Munda had no assistant, he would accomplish each and every official job of his single-handedly. Besides, he used to draft reports, circulars, letters, communiqués and replies to people's representatives at the behest of Dr Gourhari Ghosh and the officer-in-charge of the MCD. Wherever and whenever there was a need to highlight the mosquito control activities of BMC, Munda's involvement was mandatory.

These apart, he would attend the meetings of 5-6 borough committees in every month. Workshops, seminars, awareness meetings, meetings with state health department—all had to be attended by one man of the health department of BMC, Munda. But the saddest part of the story is that no transport was provided to him by Dr Gourhari Ghosh. Gourhari was a sadist. He never asked Munda about the difficulties he had been facing over the years in rendering outdoor services due to lack of a vehicle. An adept in the subject of mosquitoes adorned with the degree of PhD, Munda used to travel in buses and sometimes in a matador van. Though there was a jeep in the MCD, the service of the vehicle was uncertain. It was a very old jeep and most of the times, it would remain out of order. The driver of the vehicle was a branded supporter of PPFI. He was erratic and very sly. "No jeep, no tension" was his motive. He had a strong political back-up and hence he would not bother about his duties.

Still Munda was very happy with his official job. Having been deeply involved in almost every work of the MCD over the past 7-8 years, Munda dreamed a lot about his department and his professional career. He thought that one day he would become the officer-in-charge of the MCD. He thought antimosquito activities across the city of Beldanga would run under his administrative control. He would plan and implement mosquito control strategies himself. Nobody in the health department of BMC would interfere in his activities. He thought Gourhari Ghosh would deploy 15 more entomologists in the department (@ one entomologist for each borough of BMC) to help him work in a better way. The entire country would recognise the activities of his department. He would be able to undertake studies on mosquitoes of Beldanga independently and his research articles would be published in international journals on a regular basis. He thought he would attend international seminars and highlight the entomological activities of his department there before the scientists from different countries around the world. He thought experts from all around the country would know him by name and respect him as the country's best entomologist. And Gourhari would make him the city's chief entomologist and uplift him to a higher post so that he could run his departmental activities independently.

Munda was really working hard to begin a real fight against mosquitoes of Beldanga to prevent malaria, dengue, etc. In 1996, he formed a special surveillance team (SST) by deploying 5 volunteers of a renowned club on a contractual basis, to study the mosquitoes of Beldanga as and when required. Rigorous in-field training was imparted to the members of this team to develop their technical skill. A jeep, hired at Rs 500 per day, was provided to the SST to help it move in promptness from one place to another across the city for collecting information about mosquitoes. Needless to say, this SST was the one and only research team in the MCD at the disposal of Munda. By employing the service of this team, Munda started gathering interesting information from different corners of Beldanga about the breeding habitats of the city's malaria and dengue spreading mosquitoes—*Anopheles stephensi* and *Aedes aegypti* respectively. And within a very short span of time, the SST of Munda became very popular in the health department of BMC.

The performance of his SST was so encouraging that Munda began to think of forming two-three more such efficient teams to widen the scope of mosquito research needed to plan scientific strategies for prevention of mosquito-borne ailments in the city of Beldanga. The mercury of Munda's dream began to scale high. Plans, aspirations, imaginations and ambitions began to crowd his rustic mind.

But the dreams of this entomologist were all shattered by one single stroke of Gourhari. It was May 13 in 1997. By issuing an official order, this very autocrat stripped Munda of his supervisory power over mosquito control activities across the city and delegated the power to 15 borough executive health officers (Br Ex HOs) of BMC, putting an end to the existence of the MCD forever.

Field workers and all other categories of mosquito control staff, who had been working at Munda's behest since 1989, became the men of Gourhari's brethren overnight. Free movement of the BMC's only entomologist to different branch offices stopped. Entomological activities of Munda came to a standstill. What Munda would do in the changed administrative set-up was not clarified by Gourhari in his communiqué. The deputy CMHO, who had been working as the head of the MCD stopped coming to the department following the instructions of Gourhari Ghosh. Gourhari had asked him to do his official job sitting at the headquarters of BMC.

Two-three months later, Gourhari began deploying medical officers (MOs) in different wards of each of the 15 boroughs of BMC on a contractual basis and gave them a go-ahead to steer mosquito control activities in their wards. Munda's life came to an end. His presence in the health department became meaningless. Making an official visit to a ward of BMC to monitor the activities of an MO with regard to mosquito-bashing programme was not feasible for Munda since he and an MO are of the same official rank.

An era of mosquito control activities under the administrative control of the MEDICAL FRATERNITY began in the city of Beldanga at the behest of Dr Gourhari Ghosh. The Marxist mayor of BMC, Sushanta Chatterjee, was visibly happy with the activities of Gourhari. Creating job opportunities for so many doctors at a time by cribbing the post of one ENTOMOLOGIST was indeed a "wow" thing done by Gourhari. This was done so delicately and strategically that reversing it by anyone else would be very tough in future.

In 2000, the Proletariat Protection Front of India lost the civic election. Another political party came in to govern the BMC. The era of Gourhari came to an end. He was stripped off his power by the new board. Munda became one of the team members of Dr Ratantanu Mukherjee—the new emperor of the health department!!! Till 2005, the health department of BMC ran under the control of Dr Mukherjee and Munda served him religiously. But the basic problem of Munda remained unaddressed. Munda, our silly bastard, remained stagnant right there where he had been 5 years ago. Mukherjee did not even utter a single word against the injustice caused to Munda by Gourhari. Like Gourhari, Ratantanu too was deadly against uplifting Munda above the post of an MO. As they say, assholes come with different faces but they all are the same.

In 2005, the PPFI reemerged to a new lease of power in BMC and the old haggard, Dr Nishikanta Dey, who had most unsuccessfully run the health department during 1985 to 1990 as the MMIC (Health), again got the portfolio and sat at the helm of the BMC's health administration. Ratantanu left the department on his superannuation. An unprecedented power struggle began between two worthless Dy CMHOs—Dr Dashanan Das and Dr Jagatpati Roy—to take over the post of the chief municipal health officer. It was indeed a very gripping and entertaining show that continued for nearly 3 to 4 months. Dashanan was in chair for the first half of the day and Jagatpati took over the reins in the second half.

Activities of the health department of BMC shut down. Completely. "Who's on that chair?" was the only question which made rounds among the staff members of BMC. "Jagatpati or Dashanan?" "Dashanan or Jagatpati?" Oh! What fun the guys were having asking these two questions!!! They had found out a new game to bash away their boredom (I use this term because they do nothing basically). The new game was called 'J & D' or alternatively 'D & J'.

To put an end to the impasse, the municipal commissioner of BMC, Trilochon Bandyopadhyay, IAS, had to intervene personally. Initially, he tried to resolve the crisis amicably, but failed miserably. He then brought in a branded miscreant from the state health department—Dr Dindayal Chatterjee—and made him the chief municipal health officer of BMC. Having lost the race to such foreign body, both Dashanan and Jagatpati turned furious. But the two vile creatures had to keep themselves mum since the the idea of terminating their unprecedented tussle for chair was conceived and implemented by none other than Trilochon Bandyopadhyay himself. With the tacit support of Dr Nishikanta Dey, Dashanan Das made various attempts to dislodge Dindayal but his plans did not work.

In 2006, Dashanan Das drove the last nail into the coffin of Dr Animesh Munda. Without taking his consent, Dashanan withdrew the hired vehicle which had been used by the SST since 1996 to conduct surveillance across the city under the guidance of Munda. The sky of Munda developed another irreparable crack. The SST stopped working for Munda. To avoid political hassle, Dashanan placed the SST in a ward of BMC to work under the guidance of the ward MO. Dindayal Chatterjee was aware of this detrimental work of Dashanan but remained silent all along. After losing his last resort, Munda became absolutely helpless. His post became crippled. The life of an entomologist was finished. And all around Munda noticed his massacre as silent spectators.

Sitting in the lap of Trilochon, Dindayal left no stone unturned to siphon money from BMC. Skillful pig!!!

Till the middle of 2010, he was the king of BMC's health department. Like some other idiots of the department, Munda too allowed himself to be mesmerised by Dindayal. Relentless job rendered by those fools helped him continue his term quite successfully. Munda was five years older now. Munda had done multifarious job to uphold the image of Dindayal. But Dr Dindayal Chatterjee, like Dr Ratantanu Mukherjee, too had no will to push the chair of Munda ahead. All needed was just one push. One-push ahead.

In June 2010, by winning the civic election against PPFI, a twelve-year-old political party came to power. And Jagannath Panja became the MMIC (Health) of BMC. Munda has since then been doing multifarious job following the instructions of Mr Panja. Munda's importance in the department was highlighted to all concerned by Jagannath. Munda was given a free hand by Jagannath to improve the quality of mosquito control activities across the city. Doctors of the department were asked by him to follow Munda's instructions with regard to mosquito abatement. The entire medical fraternity of BMC began fearing him. Unfortunately, Jagannath still does not know why Munda's official rank needs an uplift. Jagannath is the man who can overshadow the horrendous and strategically made blunder by Dr Gourhari Ghosh back in 1997. He is the man who can give our man Munda the much-needed back-up to go ahead, one step. Just one step. For a staggering sixteen years, our loser has been suffering this pain silently. Sixteen long years. The ray of hope still eludes Munda. Will Panja do it for Munda? He can. But will he? Munda doesn't hope any more. He doesn't dream any more. His eyes don't have dreams in them but the insults and agonies of 16 years.

Between 30 October 2010 and 31 August 2012, three worthless Dy CMHO's—Dr Jagatpati Roy, Dr Mirzafar Mohammad and Dr Dashanan Das—by cashing in on the services of the then Dy CMHO and OSD (Health) Dr Nirjan Baker and Munda, worked as the Acting CMHO of BMC one after another. And they all enjoyed playing the role since they had nothing to do but only to sign the files prepared and placed before them by Dr Nirjan Baker and Munda. The chamber of the CMHO was an absolute PEACE HAVEN for these three cunning civic officials. Munda tried to serve them to the fullest extent but could never be a man of theirs. Munda was unknown to them. So was the story of Munda's deprivation.

Then came the period of Dr Nirjan Baker. On 1 September 2012, he became the CMHO of BMC. Munda thought he would do something to assuage his chronic pain. But he too preferred to remain quiescent. For over 15 years, Munda had regarded Nirjan as his elder brother. In front of many employees of his department, friends and relatives, Animesh Munda had boasted about Dr Baker, saying, "Nirjanda is great. Unlike Gourhari, Ratantanu, Dindayal, Mirzafar, Jagatpati and Dashanan, Nirjanda is entomologist-friendly." But all his perceptions about Nirjan came wrong. It was in the late April or early May 2013. While talking to Nirjan, Jagannath Panja asked him about the official status of Munda. Nirjan gave an evasive answer to him. Nirjan said, "Munda's salary and the salary of a deputy CMHO are the same." He did not divulge the information that Munda had obtained the benefits of CAS (Career Advancement Scheme) twice, one after completing 10 years of service and one after completing

20 years of service. Hence his salary became equal to that of a deputy CMHO. The benefits he had been given by the BMC authorities were absolutely non-promotional. The official rank of Munda's post was still akin to that of an MO. And Munda would retire from the same post. Jagannath Panja got confused by the words of Nirjan and he got an impression that he had nothing to do for Animesh Munda. Standing beside them, Munda minutely listened to the discussion between the MMIC (Health) and CMHO. Munda's idea about Nirjan changed. His eyes welled up with anger and hatred. Another enemy in disguise was unmasked by Munda. "Nirjanda, you too have stabbed me in the back." Having muttered this to himself, Munda left the chamber of Jagannath Panja.

Having taken in all humiliations and insults from the health officials of BMC over the past 24 years, Dr Animesh Munda has learnt a lot. He has no regrets in life. He has only this message to dispatch to the school students: "Don't choose entomology as your career option. And in case you do PhD on mosquitoes, don't work in any department run by doctors. Go somewhere else. The medical fraternity is genotypically entomologist-hater. Docs will make your life a hell." Basically what Animesh Munda, entomologist of BMC, wants to say, rather scream out, is: "DON'T BE ME."